A Boy Called
TWISTER

ANNE SCHRAFF

SADDLEBACK
EDUCATIONAL PUBLISHING

URBAN UNDERGROUND

SADDLEBACK
EDUCATIONAL PUBLISHING
www.sdlback.com

© 2010 by Saddleback Educational Publishing

ISBN-13: 978-1-61651-002-2
ISBN-10: 1-61651-002-1
eBook: 978-1-60291-787-3

Printed in Guangzhou, China
0212/CA21200288

16 15 14 13 12 5 6 7 8 9 10

CHAPTER ONE

Kevin Walker walked slowly onto the campus of Harriet Tubman Senior High School. The school was bigger than any other he'd ever attended. Right in front of the building was a large statue of a woman in a long dress with high button shoes and a cape. She had a determined look on her plain, kind face.

"That's Harriet Tubman," a girl offered. "Our school is named for her."

"Oh," Kevin said.

"She led a lot of slaves to freedom in the eighteen hundreds. They called it the "Underground Railroad." It wasn't a railroad though. It was a string of safe houses where the slaves hid in the daytime. The slave catchers were after them with dogs and everything. So they traveled by night and hid during the day," the girl explained with a smile. "You're a new student, huh?"

"Yeah. I just moved here from Texas. Oh, my name is Kevin Walker," Kevin said.

"I'm Alonee Lennox," the girl introduced herself. "Welcome to Tubman High. It's a good school. We got some great teachers and some okay ones. Lot of friendly kids. That's what I love about Tubman."

Kevin nodded. The girl seemed nice enough—friendly to be sure. Kevin tended to be shy, and he smiled and thanked her and then moved on. Kevin felt uncomfortable talking to people he didn't know, or maybe to anybody. Before moving to Tubman, he and his mother had lived in a small town in Texas, Spurville. His mother was a registered nurse. There were just the two of them. Kevin had gone to Spurville High School, which was about one-fourth the size of Tubman. While Tubman had trees and a nice green lawn, Spurville High was shabby without much landscaping. Still, Kevin missed it. He missed everything about Spurville. He felt like a fish out of water, having trouble breathing.

Kevin looked at his class schedule. He had English first. In Spurville Mrs. Roberts, an elderly woman, taught English. It was Kevin's favorite class. On hot days she put out a bowl of lemonade with ice floating in it, and the students were welcome to dip in and fill their paper cups. Kevin read the name of the teacher here: Mr. Pippin. He wondered what he was like. Probably he wouldn't be as nice as Mrs. Roberts.

When Kevin walked into the classroom, he felt many eyes on him. He was arriving in the middle of the school year, which was uncommon. He wasn't dressed like the other guys in the room. Instead of the new styles, he wore old jeans and a white shirt. He didn't see anybody else wearing a white shirt. Everybody else wore T-shirts. But Kevin's grandmother insisted he wear a nicely pressed white shirt.

Kevin heard snickering when he sat down. He saw three boys staring at him and laughing. Kevin's face warmed. He wished he were back in Spurville. Twenty times a day he wished that, but he couldn't go back to Spurville until he finished high school. He wouldn't have minded being here in California for a visit, but to think Spurville was not home anymore made him sick to the core of his being.

Kevin noticed the girl who told him about Harriet Tubman was in this class too. She smiled at him, and she seemed worried about him. Kevin knew who Harriet Tubman was even before Alonee explained her importance. Kevin had listened out of politeness. Kevin's mother taught him a lot of things, including the story of the "Black Moses," Harriet Tubman's nickname.

Mr. Pippin appeared at the front desk, sliding in like a gray ghost. Kevin liked him immediately. He was old and worn looking. His suit was shabby. Kevin thought he must have a lot of knowledge, like Mrs. Roberts did. Kevin and Mr. Pippin had something else in common too. Kevin was nervous being in this classroom, and for some reason Mr. Pippin seemed uneasy too.

"We will be discussing the "Rocking-Horse Winner" today," Mr. Pippin announced. "A fine story by D. H. Lawrence. Does anyone wish to start?"

A boy in the back of the room rocked back and forth in his chair, making a squeaking noise.

"Marko Lane," Mr. Pippin said, "stop that."

"I was trying to get into the mood of the story, Mr. Pippin, you know, the rocking horse," Marko replied. His friends laughed.

Kevin felt sorry for the teacher, who looked stressed. Mr. Pippin looked like an outnumbered soldier on the battlefield, bravely fighting on though he knew in the end he was doomed. Kevin was shy in social situations, but he liked to participate in class discussions. He was articulate when he had something to say. By a happy coincidence, Mrs. Roberts had introduced her English class to the "Rocking-Horse Winner" a few weeks ago in Spurville. So Kevin raised his hand.

"The story has a very powerful message about how needing more and more money can destroy people," Kevin stated.

Mr. Pippin stared at the new boy. The dead, dull look in the teacher's face flamed with a look of hope. "Yes! Give us an example of this . . ." —he consulted the roster—"Kevin."

"Well," Kevin went on. "The mother. She never felt she had enough money. She was driven to search for more. And this destroyed her son."

"The mother," Alonee added, "felt the family was unlucky because they didn't have more money."

"Yes, yes," Mr. Pippin said.

"Even the walls seemed to be crying for more money," Jaris Spain, another student, offered.

"Yes, yes," Mr. Pippin encouraged. A real class discussion was going on, and Kevin had started it.

Marko Lane moved his desk with a scraping noise. Usually that kind of antic brought laughter from his friends. But now it seemed everybody wanted to talk about the story.

"The boy in the story—Paul," Mr. Pippin interjected. "How did his mother's obsession with success affect him?"

"He like caught the disease of wanting more money for his mother's sake," Kevin answered. "He rode that wooden rocking horse in his room, and he got the names of real horses, and he bet on them and won money for his mom. And eventually he died riding that horse."

When the class ended, Kevin decided he really liked Mr. Pippin. He reminded Kevin of Mrs. Roberts. He was an interesting, intelligent man.

As Kevin walked from class, Marko

Lane stuck out his foot and made Kevin stumble. Then Marko said with exaggerated concern, "Hey, I'm sorry dude. I didn't see you."

"It's okay," Kevin muttered.

"Where you from man?" Marko asked.

"Texas," Kevin replied. He walked a little faster. He hoped to lose Marko Lane and the boys who trailed along with him.

"Texas!" Marko repeated. "I never met anybody from Texas before." He looked at his friends and asked them if they knew anybody from Texas. They shook their heads, laughing. Marko was on top of his game.

"You got a whole lot of cows down there, don't you man?" Marko asked.

"Uh, not where I lived," Kevin said.

"Then how come you smell like cow pies?" Marko asked, causing an eruption of laughter from his friends. "Not to offend you or anything dude, but I think you been spending too much time on the range."

Kevin knew they were baiting him, but he ignored them. He saw a teacher just ahead. At least he thought she was a teacher—a smartly dressed woman carrying a briefcase. He hurried to catch up to her, "Excuse me, ma'am, where's Room 24?" he asked, "I got American history there."

The woman was beautiful. She smiled at Kevin and said, "I'm going there now. I teach the class. I'm Torie McDowell. And you are—"

"Kevin Walker," Kevin responded. He glanced back and saw Marko and his friends falling back into the shadows. For some reason they seemed afraid of this woman.

"Welcome to Tubman High, Kevin. We just go around this corner and we're there," Ms. McDowell said.

Kevin took a seat in the middle of the classroom. He was glad not to see Marko Lane and his buddies. Back in Spurville, there were boys like Marko. Kevin developed a deep hatred for them. He tried to avoid them, but sometimes things got too bad. Then Kevin had to deal with them.

Once Kevin Walker almost killed a boy. He hoped it would never get that far with Marko Lane.

Kevin liked American History I. Back in Spurville, he liked most of his classes. He was not brilliant, but he was a good student and he enjoyed learning. Kevin's mother had worked hard as a nurse, but she had always made time to get books from the library for herself and Kevin. "We need to stimulate our minds all the time," she used to tell Kevin. So they read books about astronomy and archeology, as well as the biographies of famous men and women. At night, when she got home from the hospital, she would sit with Kevin. She used to say things like, "Kevin, did you know that John Adams and Thomas Jefferson both died on the same day, July 4, 1826? Isn't it amazing that they would both go like that on such an important holiday?"

Kevin had loved to hear his mother talk. She had a lilting, musical voice. She led the Voices of Praise choir at the local church.

When she sang, her voice would soar. But when she talked, her voice was soft and comforting.

Before Ms. McDowell started class, a boy came up to Kevin's desk. Kevin recognized him from Mr. Pippin's class. "I thought I heard Mr. Pippin call you Kevin," he said.

Kevin looked warily at the tall, handsome boy who stood beside his desk. Did he have a problem with Kevin? "Yeah, my name is Kevin," he replied.

"My name is Jaris Spain. I wanted you to know that we just had the best English class in ages because of you. Most times it's a zoo in there. Some of those guys really harass Mr. Pippin, but you set a good tone right away and it changed everything. I just wanted to thank you," Jaris said.

"Uh . . . thanks," Kevin murmured.

When it was time for lunch, Kevin did what he usually did in Spurville. He found a quiet spot, put his nose in a book, and read. Mom had always made wonderful sandwiches for Kevin. They were interesting, with different kinds of cheeses, condiments, and maybe a lettuce leaf and radishes or hot chili peppers. But now that Kevin was making his own lunches, they were made of salami and cheese or peanut butter and jelly. Grandma was not a good sandwich maker. "Make what you like, boy," she once told him. "I know what Grandpa likes, but I don't know what a boy like you likes."

Kevin opened his book and began eating his peanut butter and jelly sandwich. He hoped Marko Lane or somebody like that wouldn't come along to disturb his peace. Instead, a big, pretty girl with braided hair appeared. "Hi there, stranger!" she boomed. "I never seen you around Tubman before, so you must be brand new. I'm Sami Archer. And I just wanted to let you know I'm here if you need any help—if you get lost or something."

"Thank you," Kevin responded. "I'm okay."

"So what's your name, stranger?" Sami inquired.

"Kevin Walker," Kevin said.

"You're not from around here. You got a cute little twang to your voice, boy. Texas or Oklahoma. Am I right?" Sami asked.

"Texas," Kevin said.

"Well, like I said, just holler if you need anything," Sami offered, strolling off. She seemed to sense that Kevin just wanted to read his book and have lunch.

Kevin thought the girl had very beautiful eyes. They reminded him of his mother's eyes. Kevin closed his book and lay back on the grass, looking up at the sky. Clouds were tumbling around in the blue. Kevin could hear his mother's voice.

"See the cirrus clouds, baby? Firm and curly, way up high. Now your cumulus clouds, they look more like whipped cream or fluffy mashed potatoes. And the stratus, low and gray, and very serious."

Kevin missed his mother. He missed her every day and every night. Sometimes, after he went to bed at night, he cried for her like a little boy although it had been three months since she died.

Kevin had come to California to live with his grandparents—Roy and Lena Stevens—because there was no other family to take him in. Kevin's grandparents were in their seventies, and they lived in a modest little home on Iroquois Street. Kevin and his mother had come every year to visit them in California, and sometimes his grandparents had come to Spurville to visit Kevin and his mother. They had a pickup truck with a camper on the back, and the four of them traveled in that truck when they went on vacation together. In those days, his grandparents never expected that one day they would be caring for a sixteen-year-old boy. But they did their best to make Kevin feel at home.

"It's been a good long while since we had a teenager in the house," Grandma remarked. "That makes for some changes, you bet your boots boy. Been 'bout thirty years since your mama was a teenager in our house. And she was such a good girl. Quiet and wanting to study all the time. Never give us a bit of trouble. We were so proud. She was wanting to be a doctor, but there was no money for that. So she became a nurse, a registered nurse, a wonderful one. You're a lot like your mama, Kevin. Studying, quiet. Not like those crazy wild youngsters who want to be hopped up and drinking whisky and scaring the living daylights out everybody."

"Praise the Lord you're not like your daddy, boy!" Grandpa would exclaim. "All I can say is praise the Lord for that."

Kevin's mother did not speak very much about Charlie Walker, Kevin's father. She never kept the truth about what happened from Kevin either. When she spoke of Charlie Walker, she was respectful. She didn't try to sugarcoat the truth, but she refused to demonize the man.

Charlie Walker was sent to prison for second-degree murder when Kevin was three years old. He died in prison during a riot when Kevin was six.

"Your father was not a bad man," Kevin's mother said. "He was a proud man. He wouldn't be any man's fool. He had a fierce temper, and one day another man insulted him and there was a fight. The other man fell into the street and hit his head and died. It didn't matter that the other man was a bully and that he'd started the fight. Your father got ten years for second-degree murder. Well, there was a riot at that prison, and some of the guards were hurt badly. Seven of the men imprisoned there died, and your father was one of them. Just remember this, Kevin. Your father was not a bad man. He was a man who loved his family. He loved you and he loved me. He just had a very bad temper and it got the best of him that day. It was like a wild thing inside him, and he never tamed it . . ."

Whenever Grandpa Roy was thanking God that Kevin was not like his father, Kevin didn't say anything. But what Grandpa said was not entirely true. Kevin thought that a lot of his father's temper stirred in his own soul too.

Back in Spurville there were some boys like Marko Lane. They had tried to bait Kevin, just like Marko did today. Kevin avoided people like that as much as he could. Maybe his father tried to avoid fighting too. Maybe there were many days he tried to ignore the bully he eventually killed by accident. And then one day the bullying became too much.

Kevin remembered Buck Sanders from Spurville. Kevin and Buck were both thirteen, but Kevin was a bit taller and stronger. Buck could sense weakness in a person from a mile off. He learned early that Kevin was something of a loner with a lot of shyness in him. He began teasing Kevin in small ways. At first Buck snatched one of Kevin's sandwiches—the good ones his mother had made—and tossed it onto the roof of the school library. The next day he deliberately spilled half his cola into Kevin's backpack.

Then, finally, as Kevin was taking a report he had carefully written from his binder, Buck snatched it up and ran. Kevin couldn't catch him to retrieve it until Buck had torn it into many pieces and cast the pieces to the wind.

Kevin had demanded that Buck leave him alone, but Buck wouldn't. He laughed and said he wasn't afraid of Kevin. And then one day, when Kevin was walking down a dirt road leading from school on a Friday afternoon, Buck Sanders jumped out of nowhere and spat in Kevin's face.

The two boys were alone. It was a hot, dusty afternoon in June. Kevin stared at his tormentor for a long second, then lunged at him and got Buck down into the dirt. Buck struggled, but Kevin was beating him with his fists. Kevin's rage grew. Suddenly he didn't want just to beat up Buck Sanders. He wanted to do more. He needed to end the abuse forever. Kevin got his hands around Buck's throat and squeezed. Buck's eyes bugged out and filled with terror. Kevin almost killed Buck Sanders that day.

CHAPTER TWO

Kevin was standing at the beverage machine when he heard some boys laughing. He thought they were laughing at him, but he didn't turn to look. He focused on putting his coins in the machine and getting his soda. The voices floated in the air, punctuated by squeals of glee. "Did you see him go down? On the library steps. He took all his books with him!" a boy yelled. "He like lost all his books, and they went into the bushes!"

Another boy, laughter gurgling in his throat, cried, "He's such an idiot. He couldn't even find all the books!"

"And then . . . and then," Marko Lane said, gasping to breathe between bursts of laughter, "he knelt down in the mud and got brown stains all over his pants. It looks like dog turd!" The laughter exploded again. "Look, look! Here he comes!"

Kevin didn't turn. He got his soda and started away.

"Hey Derrick, how'd you get dog turd all over your pants?" Marko shouted.

"Huh?" Derrick said. "It's not turd!"

"Look at him," one of the boys screamed. "He's sniffing his pants. He thinks it *is* dog poo!"

"You guys, it's just mud," Derrick replied in a hurt voice. "What's the matter with you anyways?"

"Poor Derrick," Marko taunted. "He can't help he's stupid."

"I'm not stupid," Derrick said. "I got a C in history. Ms. McDowell says I'm doing better."

Kevin thought to himself, "Why is that guy even talking to those creeps? Why doesn't he just ignore them? Doesn't he realize that all they want to do is hurt him?" Finally, Kevin turned for a glimpse of the boy under attack. He wasn't big. He had a lean frame. He looked weak. Kevin didn't know anything about him, but he probably wasn't a great student. He was a thin, clumsy boy with poor grades—the perfect foil for bullies.

Marko and his friends were like predator animals in the brush, seeking to take down the weak prey. But animals had an excuse. All they wanted was something to eat. Marko and the others didn't have to be picking on Derrick. They did it out of pure meanness.

Kevin glanced at Derrick as he passed by. His face was blank. He wasn't showing any pain if he felt any. Maybe he was used to this kind of treatment. Maybe he had become resigned to it. Maybe it had been going on for so long he thought he deserved it. Or maybe deep in his heart he hated it, hated *them*, and hoped they would someday be eaten by vultures.

"Hi Kevin," a girl said. "How's your day going?"

Kevin turned. It was Alonee, the girl who explained to him who Harriet Tubman was. "Okay," he said to her.

"You finding all your classes? It sometimes gets confusing when you're new at a school," Alonee added.

"Yeah, I'm doing okay. Right now I'm supposed to be going to science," Kevin said.

"Me too. Come on. We can go together. You'll like science. Our teacher—his name is Mr. Buckingham and he's a big environmentalist. He just fumes about all the damage we're doing on the earth. Sometimes I think he'd like it if all the people disappeared and the world would be left to the animals," Alonee laughed.

"Well, I guess we're wiping out the animals pretty fast," Kevin remarked. "I saw a show on television that said every day a bunch of animal species disappear and it's all over for them 'cause they'll never come back."

A sad look came to Alonee's face. "I feel sorry for the little animals in my neighborhood. We used to have a lot of empty fields around here leading up to the hills. Then more houses were built, and now the animals got nowhere to go. Like the opossum, and the raccoons, and foxes. They hang out in back yards and scrounge for food. We put out food for them sometimes," Alonee said.

"Yeah," Kevin countered. "The trouble with that is, they get used to people and not everybody likes them hanging around. They think people are their friends, and then somebody shows up with a BB gun or poison."

Kevin noticed that Alonee was a very pretty girl. She seemed really nice too. She was the kind of girl he felt drawn to, but he resisted that sort of feeling. Back home in Spurville, there were girls Kevin had liked. He had wanted to take them for a pizza or down to the barbecue place. But Kevin was always afraid to get close to anybody for fear they'd ask questions he did not want to answer.

Kevin's parents were living near Hudson, Texas, when his father was sent to prison. When he died, Kevin's mother moved to Spurville and worked at a nearby hospital. Nobody in Spurville knew about Charlie Walker, and Kevin's mother preferred it that way. Kevin did too. He didn't want any questions then. He didn't want any questions now.

He would run the script of questions through his head.

"Oh, both your parents are dead?"

"Yes, both of them are dead."

"They must have died young."

"My mom died of cancer last year."

"Oh, that's so sad. She must have been young."

"Yeah, forty one."

"And your father? Was he young too? He must have been."

Kevin wouldn't lie about his father. He wouldn't invent any fairy tale that his father died a hero in some war or fell off an oil rig near Galveston. Kevin's mother never lied about the circumstances of Charlie Walker's death. Neither would Kevin. So he thought it was better that he didn't form any close relationships and didn't have to face any uncomfortable questions. He didn't want his skeletons to come tumbling out of the closet for the entertainment of people like Marko Lane or the sympathy of a girl like Alonee.

Kevin and Alonee walked into Mr. Buckingham's class together. He was, as usual, putting up scary charts marking the decline of flora and fauna all over the earth.

"Pesticides!" Mr. Buckingham shouted once the class started. "Why must we eradicate every poor, harmless weed in our gardens? Why must our lawns look so perfect? Do we not know, especially here in California, that we shouldn't even have lawns? They require too much water. We should grow native, drought-resistant plants. And if a weed has the audacity to poke its head out somewhere, why not reach down and pull the thing up with our hands? Weeding is good for your health. Don't turn your yards into war zones where you are blasting weeds with poison gas!"

Kevin found himself admiring the man's outrage. He was passionate about something important. You had to admire that in a man. Kevin glanced at Alonee, and she was nodding in agreement with Mr. Buckingham. Alonee leaned toward Kevin and whispered. "Isn't he impressive looking? He looks like a king. Mr. Buckingham's ancestors were royalty in the Songhay Empire centuries ago."

"Ms. Lennox," Mr. Buckingham said in his rolling thunder voice. "I thought I made it clear eons ago in this class that we do not chat with our seatmates when I am lecturing. However, since you are so anxious to be talking while I am talking, I invite you now to tell the class in your own words what I have been saying."

"I'm sorry, Mr. Buckingham," Alonee replied in a humble voice. "You were telling us that, if we find weeds in our yard, we should pull them up by hand and not blast them with pesticides."

"Correct," Mr. Buckingham said. "You are forgiven young lady because you apparently have the rare gift of being able to listen attentively and talk at the same time."

After class, as Kevin and Alonee were leaving, Alonee asked Kevin, "Do you play football? You look like you might."

"No," Kevin answered. "I played a little football in Texas but I wasn't good at it. The only sport I was good at was track. I'm a pretty fast runner. I love to run."

"You should join the track team, Kevin," Alonee urged. "Our coach, he's been struggling to put together a winning team. He's always looking for kids who can run or long jump. So far we've never won a meet."

Kevin shrugged. "Maybe I'll go see him." He knew that Alonee was trying to befriend him, to get him involved in school activities. Maybe she liked him. He was a big, good-looking boy. Or maybe she just felt sorry for him because he was new and not adjusted yet to Tubman. Coming to a new school with the semester well underway was hard. It was even harder if you were shy like Kevin was. Maybe Alonee saw that.

Once again it came to Kevin's mind that he could really like this girl. But he didn't want to get mixed up with anybody. One thing would lead to another, and pretty soon he'd be telling her things he shouldn't be talking about. And people like Marko Lane would find out about Kevin's father and have another reason to torment Kevin.

Kevin just wanted to finish his junior year, do his senior year here in California, and then be on his own. He figured he'd go back to Texas. He liked Texas. It was home. He liked the wildflowers and the billy goats eating the brush as they roamed through the acacia, mesquite, and mimosa. Kevin liked places like Copperas Creek with white poppies growing all over. He missed Geronimo Creek and the Guadalupe River. He wanted to stand at Woman Hollering Creek again.

He wanted to go home to Spurville, maybe because it was the last place his mom was. Maybe he had some crazy notion deep in his heart that she was still there among the wildflowers, laughing like a girl as she ran with Kevin through the fragrant fields.

Kevin and Alonee had left the campus by this time and were heading home on the same street.

"You seem very deep in thought, Kevin," Alonee remarked.

"Yeah, I guess," he murmured.

"Do you live close around here? Most of us walk or bike home, but there's a city bus that picks up some kids who live farther away," Alonee said.

"I live on Iroquois Street. I can walk or jog. I walked this morning."

"Did you notice that all the streets have the names of Native American tribes?" Alonee asked.

"No," Kevin said.

"Yeah, there's Mohican and Pequot and others too. That's because the man who laid out the subdivision years ago had some Iroquois in his ancestry. He thought so many streets are named for famous white people, there should be some for tribes. Most of the houses over there are really small, like they built in the old days." Suddenly Alonee smiled self-consciously. "I talk too much, don't I? Mom calls me a motormouth."

"Oh no, you're fine," Kevin protested. "I don't know much about this place. It's good to find out."

Kevin saw his street, and he jogged in one direction while Alonee took another. Kevin's grandfather had warned him not to loiter after school—to come home right away. "This ain't Spurville, Texas, boy," he said. "We got gangs around here. We got nasty gangs and dopeheads, and you don't want to be hanging around school after it empties out. Then's when they get you. They come crawling out of the woodwork."

As Kevin jogged down the street, he thought about the day, and he was pretty satisfied with it. Except for some razzing from Marko Lane, it had gone well. He liked all his classes and felt like he could do the work. He wasn't brilliant but he was willing to work very hard.

"You're no genius, baby," Mom often said, "but you're darn well smart enough to make your way in this world. You can graduate high school and go to college." Right now, Kevin did not want to go to college after high school. He thought he'd go back to Texas, learn a trade, and maybe be a mechanic or an electrician.

Grandpa Roy liked that idea. "We got a ton of young 'uns graduating from college who can't do a darn thing folks need doing," he lectured. "Can't fix a car, can't even fix a toilet. Kids need to train for somethin' useful. Be able to do somethin'. You be good at fixing somethin' and folks gonna beat a path to your door boy. A bunch of youngsters in white shirts and ties, and they can't do a blasted useful thing. They haven't sense enough to relight the pilot on the gas stove if it blows out."

Kevin's grandfather had been a very good carpenter. He belonged to the union and he made good money. Kevin's grandparents owned their tidy little house on Iroquois Street and had no debt to disturb their peace.

But Kevin's mother dreamed of something more for her only son. She was always filling his mind with knowledge, trying to make him curious about the world. Sometimes at night, just before he went to sleep, Kevin would see his mother's sweet oval face, her smooth, milk chocolate skin, her bright dancing eyes. He could almost see the dreams she had for him tumbling in her eyes like pinpoints of light.

Now, as he jogged, Kevin said aloud, "We'll see, Mom." Kevin looked around then. He wouldn't want anyone to see him talking to his dead mother, even though he did it fairly often. He felt like she could hear him somehow, and talking to her comforted him.

"Hey dude!" Kevin heard a strange voice when he was almost home. "I haven't seen you around before. You new in town?"

The owner of the voice was a boy like Kevin, but very well dressed. He wore a silk shirt, and gold chains hung around his neck. He had a hollow-cheeked look and circles under his eyes. He seemed sick with something that had no name.

"I'm new here," Kevin replied.

"Well, listen up. Name is B.J. Brady, and I got a lot of good stuff going on. If you need a job, plenty of change, I'm the man. Just go down to Papa's Pool Hall and ask for B.J. I'll be in touch. I'm the man around here. If you're hungry for a lotta green, I can find you what you need. Y'hear what I'm saying?"

"Okay, thanks," Kevin said. He thought about his grandfather's warning about people who came out of the woodwork. Here was one, Kevin thought.

B.J. nodded and disappeared like smoke around the side of an empty house with a sign out front that said, "Bank Owned."

Kevin continued to the little green frame house with the well-cultivated garden out front. This was where he lived. He would not mention B.J. to his grandparents.

"Got a lot of homework, boy?" Grandma asked when Kevin came in.

"Yeah. Mr. Pippin gave us some stories to read, and Ms. McDowell gave us a chapter, and I got math problems too," Kevin told him.

Grandpa was sitting in his chair reading the newspaper. He was seventy-seven years old and he had bad arthritis. Sometimes his walk was very wobbly. Grandma was always after him to use his walker, but he indignantly refused. "I am not some doddering old man," he insisted. "My daddy didn't use a walker when he was ninety years old!"

"I've got to write a report on some endangered animal for Mr. Buckingham in science too," Kevin went on.

"I can tell you where there's an endangered animal right here in this house," Grandpa snapped. "It's that cat always wanting to get under my feet. She almost made me trip this morning. I was about to

34

break her neck. She's running around all day like she's out to make me fall. Now *she*'s endangered, I'll tell you."

"Taffy don't mean no harm," Grandma sniffed. "She is just wanting to play. You got to watch your feet Roy. That's why you need to use the walker."

Good smells were floating from the kitchen—fried chicken, potatoes and onions, and fresh baked bread. Grandma was a good cook. She made pecan and sweet potato pie almost every other day.

"Meet any nice friends, Kevin?" Grandma asked.

"Yeah, a lot of the kids in my classes are nice," Kevin answered.

"Well, I'm glad to hear that," Grandma said. "I don't think folks here are as friendly as they are in Texas, but I say anywhere you go you can make nice friends if you are nice yourself. Even young folks. They aren't half bad. When I take the bus somewhere and it's crowded, why those boys get right up and offer me their seats. Maybe they're dressed funny with strange trousers and hairstyles I don't get, but they are kindhearted, and that's what matters."

Kevin glanced over at the dining room wall. He noticed a new picture on the wall, a beautiful photograph of Kevin and his mother, taken last year when they were all in Texas together. It was the last wonderful vacation they all had together.

"When did you hang that, Grandma?" Kevin asked.

"Just today boy," Grandma said. "It's so pretty, don't you know. You are such a handsome boy and my Ciana is so beautiful, like a young girl. She's past forty in that picture, but she could be just a girl. I just feel good to have the picture there. It makes her feel closer to me. Do you like it, Kevin?"

"Yeah, Grandma, it's beautiful," Kevin said. He had a photograph of his mother in his wallet and he looked at it often. The photograph on the wall both touched his heart and caused him pain. She looked so healthy there. It hardly seemed possible that she had just eight months to live when that picture was taken. They were all so happy that day, as they barbecued ribs along the Guadalupe River.

Kevin also had a photograph of his father in his wallet. His dad was a handsome man. Kevin looked very much like him, except for his eyes. Kevin had his mother's eyes. Kevin's father was big and broad shouldered, and he had a wide, smiling face. He was about twenty when the picture was taken. Another nice picture was never taken of him. From then on, all the pictures were taken by the police.

Kevin's memories of his father were hazy. He was a big, jovial man who carried Kevin on his shoulders and often sang songs like "Ol' Man River" in a deep, rumbling voice. When Kevin looked at the photograph, he felt sad, but not heartbroken.

Looking at his mother's picture was different. It broke his heart.

CHAPTER THREE

Coach Alphonsus Curry had never seen his Tubman Titans track team win a meet. They had come close a few times, but there was still no victory. He had some pretty good runners on the team this year. Marko Lane was the best, with Trevor Jenkins a close second. On Tuesday morning a tall, well built junior approached Curry.

"Hi. I'm Kevin Walker, and I belonged to the track team back home in Texas. Is there a chance I could join the team here?" he asked.

Curry looked the boy over. "I'm always interested in good athletes. After gym class, come on over to the field and let me time you," he said.

"Okay," Kevin said. Alonee had put the idea of joining the team in his head. Kevin didn't enjoy any other sports, and he loved running. He was pretty good at it too.

When Kevin showed up at the track field after gym, he was surprised to see Alonee standing there. She gave him a high five as he walked by. "Good for you! You're trying out," she cheered.

Coach Curry stood on the sidelines as Kevin ran around the track. Back in Spurville, Kevin learned a lot about running. He learned to run with open hands. Making fists brought tension into the whole body and slowed a runner down. Kevin ran leaning forward, improving his speed. He even learned how to breathe properly so that he wouldn't be gasping halfway through the race. Coach Podyard at Spurville High had poor equipment and a dirt track, but he understood the sport and Kevin learned a lot from him.

"Okay, that's good," Curry said, as Kevin finished the trial run. He didn't want to overpraise the boy, but he was clearly excited. Curry had never seen so much speed in a boy. Kevin was way faster than Curry's best runner, Marko Lane. "Very good, Kevin. I'll give you the schedule for team practice. Get in as much running as you can. I think you'll fit in with the team real well, son."

When Kevin showed up for the first practice, he noticed Marko Lane standing there with a smirk on his face. "Oh boy, real competition here," he laughed. "I bet you chased plenty of cows back in Texas."

"We're going to do a mile today," Coach Curry said. "Four laps. I've got six boys lined up, and I want you guys to do your best so that I can see what we've got going for us here."

Usually Marko Lane won the mile, coming out fast and leaving the other boys well behind. Trevor Jenkins usually came in second, but today he was determined to do better. He'd been doing his stretching exercises and he felt strong.

"Get ready, get set—*go!*" Coach Curry shouted, blowing his whistle.

Marko took off fast, as he always did. He had long legs. Trevor was second, and Kevin was back at sixth place. Marko noticed this and laughed. The Texas guy was even more of a jerk than Marko thought he was. He was making a fool of himself, a couple hundred feet behind the leaders after the first lap. But at the second lap, Kevin passed two boys. He was now in fourth place. Trevor had dropped to third, and Marko was still in the lead. When the third lap started, Kevin began to gain speed. He passed Trevor and the second-place runner, and he was soon just behind Marko. As the final lap came, Marko was worried. He pushed himself as he'd never done before. He couldn't bear for this Texas yokel to make him look bad.

To his horror, Marko watched Kevin sprint past him, seemingly without effort, sailing across the finish line. Marko had used every ounce of his strength to try to

41

stay ahead of Kevin, but he failed. After Kevin won, Marko leaned over to him and whispered, "You Texas turd, you'll never do this to me again! I swear it!" Nobody but Kevin heard his comment. Kevin said nothing. He turned away as a smiling Coach Curry approached him.

"Whoa, Kevin, you can run boy! That was impressive," the coach told him. "You are a member of the Tubman Titans now. We'll get you suited up so you're ready for the next meet."

Trevor Jenkins, who finished third, came up to shake Kevin's hand. "Man you go," he said. "Only time I ever ran near that fast was when my mama was chasing me with a frying pan for coming home late from school. You hear what I'm saying dude?"

Kevin smiled. "Thanks. I've done a lot of running for fun. There's a special high in just going all out," he said.

"Man, your arms were really swinging. You were a blur man!" Trevor remarked.

"Yeah, my coach in Texas told me that the faster your arms swing, the faster your legs go," Kevin replied.

Alonee came over then, a big smile on her face. "You were pretty awesome, Kevin. When you said you loved to run, I was expecting a so-so runner. You blew me away. Marko Lane looked like he'd been hit by a cement truck or something. I bet he didn't take it too well either," she commented.

Kevin shrugged. He didn't repeat Marko's slur.

That day, Kevin jogged home from school as usual. He moved at a slow, steady pace. Sometimes he listened to music as he ran, but mostly he liked to hear the natural sounds of the fields he ran through. When he ran in Texas, he could hear a lot of bird sounds.

When Kevin was halfway home, he noticed that another boy was behind him. He didn't know the boy's name, but he remembered him from Mr. Pippin's class.

Every time Marko did something stupid, this guy and a couple others would laugh. He was part of Marko's cheering section.

"Hey dude," the boy called out to Kevin.

Kevin slowed and turned around. "Yeah. What's going down?"

"I'm Tyron Becker," the boy said. "I'm a friend of Marko's. We hang out a lot. We go back to grade school. Know what I'm saying?"

"Okay," Kevin acknowledged.

"You really made Marko look bad in that race. Marko has a lot of pride, and it was kind of dirty how you played that. You hung back and waited for your chance, and then you came on like a racehorse. You kinda tricked Marko into not doing his best and that wasn't cool, y'know?" Tyron said.

"That's how I run the mile man," Kevin replied. "I don't come out flying. I gradually gain. I ran the kind of a race I was trained to run. I didn't pay any attention to what kind of race he was running. When I run, I feel like I'm all alone out there."

"Yeah, well, it didn't look good," Tyron advised. "I just want to give you a heads-up man. Marko has a lot of friends at Tubman. He's really popular. I mean, he's the man around here. If you start playing dirty against Marko, you'll have the whole school against you and I don't think you want that. You're a stranger dude, and we stick with our old friends around here."

"Okay," Kevin said. "I haven't been at Tubman long, but I've already seen a lot of Marko Lane. He does his best to cause trouble in most of the classes. He really baits Mr. Pippin in English, scraping his chair, getting phony coughing spells. And you guys are laughing like it's funny to torment a teacher. And then when some poor guy took a fall at the library, there was Marko, leading you guys in ridiculing him. I guess stuff like that makes a guy popular, but it's not my business. I'm a stranger here, yeah. I do my own thing. And I run my own race."

Tyron's eyes narrowed. "Dude, you got bad attitude. It's not gonna help you around Tubman. We're tight. We look out for our brothers, and that's what Marko Lane is, a brother," Tyron threatened.

"I thought we were all brothers man," Kevin snapped. "My grandma, she says we're all brothers. Not just me and my friends. Everybody. Mr. Pippin, he's our brother too. He's old and everything, but he's still our brother. That guy who tumbled down the library steps and got all muddied up, the guy you mocked when he was hurting. He's our brother too."

"You just watch your back man," Tyron warned bitterly.

Kevin just stood there and watched Tyron turn and walk away. Kevin knew he'd gone too far. He should have just listened to what Tyron had to say and then let it go. It might have even been wise to nod and say that he appreciated the warning. He might have agreed that Marko Lane seemed like a leader around the school and that he would try to avoid crossing Marko. But somehow all the wrong words came out—words that were from Kevin's heart, not his head.

Kevin didn't know all the exact details of the crime that got his father sent to prison. All he knew was that a man insulted Charlie Walker and there was a fight. Maybe the cause was just a conversation— like Kevin's with Tyron just now—that went bad. Kevin didn't know who threw the first punch. He knew who threw the last one.

What Kevin did know was that he had a temper too—a bad temper, like his father's. He might have killed Buck Sanders that day when he was only thirteen years old. Kevin drew back from that terrible cliff edge at the last minute that day. Now Kevin knew he must never get to that point again because he might not be able to draw back.

When Kevin was eating lunch the next day, Alonee came to join him. She introduced him to some other friends too. "These are my posse," she announced. "This is Sami Archer."

"Yeah, we know each other already," Kevin nodded.

"He the strong, silent type," Sami said with a grin. "He don't have much to say, but I'm hearing on the grapevine that this boy can run. Coach Curry is getting down on his knees now every night, thanking the good Lord for sending Kevin his way."

"This is my friend Sereeta Prince," Alonee went on, as a beautiful doe-eyed girl sat down and smiled at Kevin. Finally a lean, handsome young man joined them. "This is Jaris Spain. He acted in a school play last month, and he was fabulous."

Kevin looked at the group that formed around him. Back in Spurville he had two friends, neither of them very close. Now he had quite a group already. Trevor Jenkins showed up and told everybody, "You guys, you can't believe how fast this guy runs. This Texas stranger left Marko Lane in the dust!"

"You know," Jaris Spain said, "the sports department gives an award every year to our best athlete—the Arthur Ashe

Award for Excellence. And lately we've had trouble finding kids who earned it. It looked like Marko would win this year because he's been the fastest on the track team and pretty good in football too, but now maybe you'll get it Kevin. I'd sure love to see somebody other than Marko get it. Character counts in the award, and he's not doing so well in that department."

"It'd be a joke if Marko won it," Sami said grimly. "It'd be an insult to Arthur Ashe!"

"Yeah," Jaris said. "You know, when I was a little kid, every day my mom would pack one of those beautiful, big, seedless oranges in my lunch bag. I don't remember what they were called but they were awesome."

"Navels," Sereeta said. "They're the best ever."

"Yeah," Jaris continued, "and I really looked forward to that orange, and then one day Marko said if I didn't give it to him, he'd hurt me bad. I was kinda small and skinny then, and I was afraid of him. I gave him my orange every day. It made me so freakin' mad I felt like screaming, but I was afraid of the bully."

"We all were afraid of him," Trevor added. "Some of us still are."

"But you know," Jaris said, "I was afraid to tell my mom what was going on because she would have marched over to Marko's parents' house and made a big deal of it, and it would've been all over school that wimpy little Jaris went whining to mommy to make sure he got his orange back. And Marko would have really gotten even then. He used to threaten me that, if I crossed him, he'd find a rattlesnake and put it under my bed at night."

"Then I found out what was going on," Alonee interjected, "and I told Jaris's father. I'd see that nice big orange disappearing every day in that creep's hands, and I had to do something."

"Well, Pop has his own way of handling stuff," Jaris remembered with a smile. "He didn't go whining to Marko's parents. He puts on a red wig and a fake beard, and one day, when Marko was out shooting baskets, he comes along and tells him my big oranges had magic seeds in them. They'd grow inside Marko, and branches and leaves would come out of his ears and his mouth. Marko was like seven, and he got *scared*. Pop told him to drink a lot of cod liver oil to wash away the seeds he'd already swallowed, but never to eat another one. For weeks Marko kept watching me eat my oranges and waiting for branches to come popping out of my ears!"

"There's somebody like Marko in every school," Sereeta commented. "They got this way of knowing who to pick on. I don't know what anybody can do about it. I worry, though. I worry about the kids who get bullied. Some of them can't or won't fight back and sometimes they like explode . . ."

"Marko better watch out," Trevor remarked. "Some day he's going to bully the wrong guy, and then he'll be sorry."

Kevin focused on his peanut butter and jelly sandwich and said nothing. He avoided Trevor's gaze. Of course, Trevor had no way of knowing Kevin's past. Nobody at Tubman knew about Kevin's father. And nobody knew how close Buck Sanders came to dying that Friday afternoon.

When the others drifted away, Kevin thought about Buck Sanders again. As soon as he was spat upon that day, Kevin knocked Buck down and started pounding on him with his fists. Buck struggled to get up, but he couldn't. Somehow, between blows, he was able to scream at Kevin, "You leave me alone or you're in big trouble."

But Kevin kept on pounding him in the face and the body. Buck cursed him, and then Kevin put his hands around the other boy's neck and squeezed. Buck's eyes widened, and he looked as though he knew he was about to die. And if Kevin had continued, he would have died. But Kevin yanked his hands back, and Buck lay there gasping and coughing as Kevin walked away. Buck understood what almost happened. He knew that he had almost been murdered, that his beaten and strangled body would have been found in the morning when the sun came up.

Kevin stumbled toward home that day. He stopped at a tree and vomited. He was shaking and covered with perspiration. He felt weak, scared, and, in a strange way, triumphant. Buck Sanders never bothered him again. They continued to be students at the same school, but they never spoke a word to one another. They passed one another like unseen ghosts.

But Trevor Jenkins did not know any of that when he said Marko Lane better be careful, or he might torment the wrong guy and pay the consequences.

"So what's your time for the two-hundred-meter dash, Kevin?" Trevor asked, drawing Kevin aside after school.

"Well, back in Texas I did it in twenty-one-four," Kevin answered, meaning 21.4 seconds.

"Oh man, that's awesome dude!" Trevor said. "What do you do to stay conditioned?"

"The usual, run, stretch, stuff like that. I eat good. My grandma is a good cook. Grandpa too. I drink a lot of milk," Kevin replied. He hadn't intended to mention his grandparents. He knew it would lead to questions.

"You live with your grandparents?" Trevor asked.

"Oh yeah. The school in Texas wasn't that good, so, uh, we decided I'd live out here with my grandparents for the rest of high school. It was good that they live here in California. Schools got modern computers and stuff. Spurville is a little town, kind of behind the times. My grandparents, they're great and it's all working out," Kevin explained. He didn't want to talk about his mother being dead. He didn't want anybody feeling sorry for him.

"Well, we're sure glad you're here," Trevor said.

On his way home from school that day, Kevin felt pretty good. He wasn't looking for friends. He was trying to keep a low profile. But still he enjoyed the gang Alonee called her "posse." He liked Sami and Sereeta, Jaris and Trevor. They were friendly and comfortable to be with. Even though he never admitted it, Kevin was feeling a little lonely in Spurville after his mother died. He had no close friends. She was the only emotional attachment he had had there. Now he felt better.

CHAPTER FOUR

When Kevin got home and Grandma asked him if he had met any nice friends, he could truthfully say that he had. "Alonee Lennox, she introduced me to her friends, Grandma, and I like them all."

"Alonee," Grandma cooed the name. "Now that sounds like the name a pretty girl would have, if I do say so."

Yeah," Kevin agreed. "She's pretty. But what really makes her special is that she's so warm. She makes me feel like I've been going to that school for a long time."

Grandpa looked up from his newspaper. He'd been working a crossword puzzle. "She cotton to you boy? Good-looking boy like you. I bet she's looking you over pretty good, eh?" Grandpa chuckled.

"Oh, she's nice to everybody," Kevin answered, his face warming.

"But maybe she's extra nice to you boy. I 'member when I was a young buck down there in Texas, and this pretty little gal came along and she set her bonnet for me pretty quick. I wasn't no wrinkled up old man with bad legs like I am now. Oh no. I was smooth and handsome as you are, Kevin. And this little gal, she was pretty as a sunflower. She's old now too, and she don't look like she did then, but I still love her plenty," Grandpa said.

Grandma Lena came back at him. "Don't you be calling me old, old man. You watch your mouth."

"Well, y'are. You're old, Lena. Ain't no sin in that," Grandpa responded firmly. "What's good is that we're still together. I never hankered to divorce you, Lena. Never wanted to trade you for another gal, though some of these bold women came on to me. I was doing carpenter work in their homes, and they'd hang around all gussied up and sweet smelling of lilac water. But I never wanted to divorce you, Lena."

"Well, I've wanted to kill you a few times, old man," Grandma said. "But I never did and more's the pity 'cause now I'd have a peaceful life." Grandma then smiled toward Kevin and said, "You can have this Alonee over anytime, honey boy. I'll cook up an extra nice meal, and if that old man over there will shave and shower and put on a clean shirt, we won't be an embarrassment to you."

"Thanks, Grandma, but we're just school friends now," Kevin explained. "Oh and another thing. I joined the track team at school. I'm a Tubman Titan now, and I get to wear the yellow and blue. Coach Curry had me run against some other guys and I won."

"Well, good for you, Kevin," Grandma said. "You were always as fast as the wind. When you were a little shaver, you'd be running all over the place, and your mama would laugh and say you went so quick she could hardly make you out. She had a nickname for you—Twister. She said the onliest thing faster than you was a twister, a Texas tornado."

"I remember her calling me Twister," Kevin recalled. "She'd have a chore for me and she'd look for me and I'd be gone. 'Come back here, Texas Twister,' she'd holler. She always called me that . . . always . . ."

The sadness came back, rolling over Kevin like a cold fog. Kevin remembered Mom in the hospital bed at hospice, where people went to die as comfortably as possible. The nurse was at her bedside all the time. Mom said, "Nurse, I want to see my boy. Twister, you haven't run off again, have you?" And Kevin, who spent almost all his time there, came to her bedside. "I'm here, Mom," he said softly. Then, when the end was very near, the hospice nurse told Kevin that, even when his mother seemed to be gone—even after she had breathed her last—he should lean close and tell her that he loved her, and she would hear him. The nurse said she would sail right into paradise with his words in her ear. And that's what Kevin did. He leaned close and said over and over, "Mama, I love you."

"Baby," Grandma remarked now, "you look troubled."

"No, no," Kevin responded. "I'm good."

"It's because I talked about your mother. It made you sad. I shouldn't talk about her so much, but I loved her and I want to remember her," Grandma explained.

"Grandma, it's okay," Kevin said. "I want to remember her too. I never want to forget her."

Grandma smiled. "I made meatloaf and mashed potatoes with thick gravy and pecan pie, sweetie," she chuckled.

"When I'm coming home from school, Grandma, I smell the good smells coming from here and I run even faster," Kevin said.

The next day, as Kevin walked onto the Tubman campus, a girl with cornrow braids said to him, "Hey, you really run fast. You're fun to watch."

"You must have seen me yesterday," Kevin replied. A small group of Tubman students watched yesterday's trial race.

"Yeah, you blew away the competition," the girl said. "Hey, I'm Carissa Polson. I think we're in the same speech class."

Just then Grandpa's old pickup truck came rolling up to Tubman. Grandma was driving. "Hey Twister," she called. "You got out so fast this morning you clean forgot your lunch."

Kevin ran to the cab and got the brown bag from his grandmother. "Thanks, Grandma. Sorry you had to come over here."

"I'm going to the supermarket anyways," Grandma said, waving from the cab of the pickup as she drove off.

"That your grandma, huh?" Carissa inquired.

"Yeah. She brought my lunch. I forgot it this morning."

"She called you Twister. What's that about?" Carissa asked.

"Texas tornadoes are called twisters. My mom gave me that nickname 'cause I'm so fast," Kevin explained.

"That's cool," Carissa commented. "You sure ran like a tornado yesterday. We're having a meet against Lincoln pretty soon. We always get buried. But if you run like I saw you, we maybe got a chance to get some points. That would be so amazing."

"I'll try," Kevin promised. Carissa was really cute. She had a dazzling smile and big brown eyes. If Kevin were not avoiding getting involved with anybody, he would have talked a little longer. But he smiled and headed for English.

Carissa said to his back, "I'm glad you came to Tubman, Twister. You make it more exciting around here."

Kevin practiced hard with the Tubman track team. Back in Spurville, practice was held on the blacktop of the school parking lot. Most of the other members of the

Spurville team were really poor, but Kevin learned the basics. He learned how to breathe deeply and smoothly and how to pace himself.

Other than Kevin, only three boys on the Tubman team were good runners. Marko Lane was good, and so was Trevor Jenkins. The third boy was a gangly kid named Matson Malloy. Coach Curry planned to build the team around these four boys.

"You guys will be in the relay team when we go against Lincoln," Curry explained. "You've all had some experience in running relays, and you know how important coordination is. The last time we ran in a relay match, we got hammered because one of the guys fumbled the baton handoff. That killed us. To be more specific, Marko, you dropped the ball that day."

Trevor and Matson laughed a little, but Kevin kept a straight face. He didn't want to antagonize Marko.

"Of the four of you, I've got to pick the fastest guy to be the anchor running the final lap. From what I've seen over these practice days, my job is easy. I'm giving the anchor position to Kevin Walker," Curry announced.

"Hey Coach," Marko spoke up, "I can help the team a lot as anchor. I'm much better than I was that day against Garfield. I really think I've earned—"

"Walker is going to anchor the team," Coach Curry said.

Kevin could feel Marko's resentment burning against him. He ignored it as Coach Curry started practice. The trial relay would be run with Trevor leading off, Marko doing the second lap, Matson the third, and Kevin doing the final lap. Coach Curry stood watching as the team took off. Trevor ran a good first lap, ahead of his usual time, and he passed the baton smoothly to Marko. Marko ran his lap better than anything he had done before, putting the team ahead of its best time. But then the baton was bobbled between Marko and Matson, almost falling to the ground. A groan went up from the little group of students watching.

"Idiot!" Marko hissed at Matson, who looked stricken. Matson managed to recover the baton and run a fair lap, but the team was well behind its best time now. By the time Matson passed the baton to Kevin, the practice run was clearly going terribly. But then, baton in hand, Kevin burned up the track. In the final push, Kevin's arms were pumping like a machine, and his body was a blur. Kevin made up the lost seconds and sailed over the finish line with a torrid time of 46 seconds. An awed silence followed, then an explosion of cheers. The spectators screamed and jumped up and down. The chant went up quickly.

"Twist-er! Twist-er! Twist-er!"

Matson Malloy came over to Kevin and said, "You're the man." Trevor gave Kevin a high five. Coach Curry was grinning widely, "That was some show, boy. You are greased lightning. I don't know what possessed your family to send you to

Tubman, but I owe them!" Curry beamed, slapping Kevin on the back.

Marko Lane was a lonely figure standing by himself. He was a good runner. Before Kevin came, he was the best of the Tubman Titans. Whatever successes the team had they owed to him. Coach Curry often said that, if the rest of the team was as good as Marko, they would win some meets. But now, suddenly, it looked like the team had found a star who could lift them to a winning and maybe even a championship season.

Slowly, Marko approached Kevin. "You think you're the big dog now, don't you? You think you've chased old Marko Lane out of the 'hood, don't you? Well, listen up, this is only the beginning," he warned.

"I'm sorry nobody ever taught you sportsmanship," Kevin replied. "We've got to work together, not against each other if we're going to be any good."

But Marko was already gone, in search of Matson Malloy. "Hey freak," he said bitterly, giving Matson a nasty shove.

"I passed the baton cleanly and you fumbled it. What are you, stupid? A monkey could have grabbed the baton, but you're not as smart as a monkey. What are you doing on the team anyway? You're a freak, you know that?"

Matson stood there, shaken. He was a gaunt, nervous boy who had never excelled in anything. But now he was a pretty good runner and he was getting better. Coach Curry was bringing him along, and the coaching was showing results. In recent weeks he had gained speed and confidence. Until today, Matson was feeling a little better about himself.

Kevin watched the ugly scene unfolding. The old rage he felt at the sight of a bully in action was roused again in his heart. He wanted to go over there and deck Marko, to push his face into the dirt. But he knew that would get him thrown off the team, and it wouldn't do Matson any good either. So Kevin just stood there until Marko had spent his fury.

Matson sat down on a tree trunk where a big eucalyptus had been sawed down. His head was bowed.

Kevin walked over and stooped near the other boy. "Hey man, it's easy to bobble the baton," he told the boy.

"Nah, it was my fault," Matson whined. "Lane was right. I'm a stupid idiot. I'm a jackass." His voice was raw and wounded.

"Matson, did you ever hear of Wilma Rudolph?" Kevin asked.

"Oh sure. She was a legend. When I joined the track team, I read all about the great runners. She won an Olympic gold medal. She was beautiful too," Matson said.

"Do you think Wilma Rudolph ever bobbled the baton during a relay race, Matson?" Kevin asked.

Matson shook his head vigorously. "No way! Not her. She was one of the best. Only dumb idiots like me fumble the baton." Matson was parroting Marko's cruel insults, believing them himself. Kevin figured this wasn't the first time somebody had told Matson he was stupid and clumsy. He had probably gotten that message most of his life.

"The Olympics, nineteen-sixty, in Rome," Kevin started. "The big relay race was on. Wilma and her three teammates were running for the United States against Russia. Everything was going great until Wilma fumbled the baton. Almost dropped it. Yeah, she did, Matson. But she was the anchor. So she ran the final lap with incredible speed and won the gold medal for the team."

"She . . . she was a champion. Champions don't fumble the baton," Matson protested, his eyes wide.

"Yeah, she did. We all do. But we learn from it and we go on. You'll learn from it and next time you'll be much better. You might even help Tubman win a meet down the road man," Kevin said.

A slow grin came to Matson's face. "Hey Twister," he said, "you're all right."

"You're all right too, Matson," Kevin came back, high-fiving the other boy.

As Kevin was heading for the street and the jog home, Carissa came along. She had obviously been waiting for him to finish talking to Matson. "That was the most exciting relay race I've ever seen," she said. "It looked dismal and you pulled it off. So tell me about yourself, Kevin. Are your parents good at sports? Do you have brothers and sisters in sports? I mean, I just want to know everything."

"I'm an only child, and my parents never got into sports," Kevin offered, hoping that closed the door to any more questions about him.

"So how did you get into running?" Carissa asked.

"I don't know. It's fun. I've always done it. I guess I never stopped," Kevin said. "Don't you run?"

"I used to, as a kid," Carissa answered. "I guess I stopped when I was ten or something. It didn't seem cool. I mean, now if I see somebody running, I think they stole something, and in a minute I'll see a clerk or the cops after them. I guess you come from a small town in Texas, but we're near a big city and we got a lot of gangs and crime."

"Well, I jog home from school, and I run across some fields, and it's nice. I even get to see the wildflowers. Running is great, it really is. Back home, my health teacher, she said that when you run for fifteen or twenty minutes, your body produces something called . . . uh, endo . . . uh, endorphins. Yeah, and they make you feel good. It's like some guys do drugs for that feeling, but you can get it just from running."

"Wow, that's really cool!" Carissa exclaimed. "I've never heard that before. Like when you're depressed you can just run it off."

"Something like that," Kevin nodded. "Well, gotta get home. See you tomorrow, Carissa."

Kevin was a little late getting home and his grandmother was worried. "You got that cell phone, boy. It ain't just for tweedling or twirping or whatever you kids do. It's also for calling your grandma and putting her mind at ease," Grandma chided.

"Sorry, Grandma. We had track practice and I did really well. Then this girl stopped me and we got to talking. I lost track of time," Kevin explained.

"This girl was Alonee? The girl you mentioned?" Grandma asked.

"No this girl's name is Carissa," Kevin replied.

"Carissa," Grandpa said, repeating the name. "Boy has been in school a coupla weeks and already he's got Alonee and Carissa. You're doing okay boy." Grandpa finished his crossword puzzle. He always used to do them in ink. Lately he was using pencil. Now he chuckled, "Lena, we got us a boy who is attracting the ladies."

"Well Kevin, you are a fine looking boy," Grandma said, "and if you run as good here as you did back home, you might end up being a big sports star, and then the girls will be wanting your autograph."

"Well, I haven't helped my team win a meet yet, but we've got one coming up against Lincoln in a few weeks. Coach Curry thinks I can compete in the hundred meters and the relay race. If we get enough points, Tubman can win for the first time in ages," Kevin said.

"Your father was good in sports, you know," Grandpa said. "He was on his way to being world champion."

Kevin spun around and stared at his grandfather. "Say what?"

Grandma glared at Grandpa. Her look said, "We don't talk about that man around here. Our daughter married a troubled man, and we don't heap praise on his head in this house. We don't even mention him."

But the words were out. They could not be called back.

Grandpa shrugged. He was sorry. But it was too late.

"Grandpa, what are you talking about?" Kevin demanded, going to the old man's chair and standing in front of him. "Nobody ever told me this before. My father was on his way to becoming world champion in *what*?"

Grandma shook her head. "Well, since the cat has jumped out of the bag—thanks to you, old man—we got no choice but to talk about the thing," Grandma conceded.

"He was a fighter, a boxer," Grandpa explained. "He was a light heavyweight. He was just a boy when he won all these preliminary fights. He was on his way to qualify for the United States Olympic team . . ."

CHAPTER FIVE

What happened?" Kevin asked.

"It was all before he and your mother got married," Grandma went on. "Your father had this bad temper, like a fire burning in him. He got into a fight, and, being a boxer, it went hard on boxers who brawled in the street. His hands were considered deadly weapons. He didn't get no jail time, but his boxing career was over. He never got to compete in the Olympics."

"He won plenty boxing matches before that," Grandpa added. "There were glossy pictures of the refs holding up his hand in victory. Thrilling pictures."

"I never saw those pictures," Kevin said. "Any of them still around?"

Grandpa looked guiltier for having brought the whole subject up. Grandma shrugged and disappeared into her bedroom. She came out with a yellow envelope. "Your mother kept some of them. When she died . . . she asked me to take care of the stuff in the cedar box," Grandma explained. "This is all there was."

"Thanks, Grandma," Kevin said, taking the envelope and going into his room.

Kevin opened the envelope and found about a dozen glossy photographs of a handsome young man in boxer's shorts. Kevin saw his own facial features in the man's eyes, his nose, even his chin. Kevin's father was smiling happily as his hand was held aloft in triumph. Seeing his twenty-year-old father in his prime was a little like looking at himself in a few years.

There were newspaper stories too, but the paper was yellowed and fragile. Kevin read the headline "Local Boy Heading for the Olympics." The story described the terrific young Charlie Walker, who was destined for Olympic glory. Other newspaper articles described preliminary fights that turned into awesome knockouts in the early rounds.

Kevin returned to the front room. He looked at his grandfather first. "Thanks Grandpa for talking about my father. It means a lot to me to have this," he said. Then he turned to his grandmother. "Thanks for keeping this stuff Mom gave you, Grandma. I know how you felt about my dad, and you might have tossed it all but you didn't. I had only one picture of him, and now all this other stuff . . . it's good."

"I'm glad it comforts you, sweetheart," Grandma told him. "You know, your mama and I, we never wanted you to look up to him because of what happened. His life had such promise, but it came to such a sad place. We were angry at him for bringing so much sorrow to this family."

"But thanks for keeping the pictures, Grandma," Kevin repeated.

"Yes. For all the wrongheaded things he did, Charlie Walker was still your father.

It didn't seem right to throw away all those shiny pictures of what he used to be," Grandma mused.

Kevin returned to his room with the pictures. He had a special place in his dresser drawer for important things like school awards from Spurville, the little trophies he won there in track for doing the 200-meter dash in 21.40 seconds and for helping win a relay. His childhood pictures were there too, of him and his mother and grandparents during wonderful times.

Before putting the pictures of his father away in the special place, Kevin wondered again what drove him to that fateful fight that sent him to prison and to his death there. Kevin probably would never know the details, but he thought it had to be like that hot day in Texas when Kevin went after Buck Sanders.

At school the next day, Kevin had lunch with Alonee and Sami. This time Kevin had made himself a good sandwich with ham and cheese and lots of relish.

"Boy, you are fly around here," Sami told him. "You notice the chicks givin' you the eye? You are the 'next big thing,' Kevin. Used to be a lotta girls would be eyeballin' Marko, and he could just about ask any girl to go with him, and she'd jump at the chance. But he's yesterday's news, now. You're the man, Kevin."

"That's not me," Kevin replied. "I don't like a lot of attention."

"That makes you all the even more fly 'cause you're not lookin' for it dude," Sami explained.

"It helps that you're nice too," Alonee added. "I was talking to Matson Malloy last night on the phone, and he told me how you talked to him and made him feel better. That was so nice. He felt so totally awful about fumbling the baton, even though it was as much Marko's fault as his. Marko made him feel terrible. I don't know how much you know about Matson, Kevin, but he's a foster kid. He got picked up by child protective when he was like six, and he's been in five different homes. His counselor told him to get into running to build his self-esteem, and it's really helped, but that thing with the baton and Marko being so ugly almost derailed him. But you fixed it, Kevin." Kevin had guessed Matson came from a hard background. Because Matson had been kicked around so much, he readily accepted Marko's abuse.

"I wouldn't have told you about Matson's past," Alonee went on, "except that Matson tells everybody. He's very honest. Marko knows about him too. That makes what he did even worse."

"Marko is such a slime," Sami commented. "His mama, she works hard in that house cleaning business she's got. She seems like she loves Marko. Marko's father, he's a range dog. He's an operator. Always got him a con going, and he's loaded with money. He's really generous with Marko. I see some new shirts and slacks in the Sunday ads and next thing I know, Marko is wearing them. Hardly anybody at Tubman dresses as good as him. Marko's daddy gets him all the hot electronics too. He got the newest gadgets before anybody else knows they're out there. Like Marko got a lot going for him, and he's still gotta be so mean."

"Maybe his daddy don't set such a good example," Alonee wondered. "Strutting around the streets with his diamond earrings and his gold chains."

"But that shouldn't make Marko so mean girl," Sami said. "He gets off on hurting people, like Matson and that poor old teacher, Pippin. Pippin goin' downhill anyway. Why does Marko need to kick him?"

Kevin remembered Buck Sanders. He would have a look of pure joy on his face when he hurt someone. When he tossed Kevin's sandwich on the library roof and he saw Kevin looking at it, he laughed crazily. When Buck hid the scorpion in Kevin's gym shoe, it seemed Buck would choke from laughing. In his thirteen-year-old mind, Kevin couldn't understand how Buck got such pleasure from hurting and scaring other kids. And in the end, Kevin stopped caring why Buck was how he was. All Kevin wanted to do was hurt him back.

"Anyway Kevin," Alonee said, "I just wanted you to know that you helped a guy who really needed a hand up, and there's icing on the cake. Matson is going to do a book report on Wilma Rudolph's life now."

In the days ahead, Kevin noticed that Marko Lane was running a lot more in practice. He seemed to be almost fanatical about his training. He was determined to build his muscles and gain enough speed to outperform Kevin. He wanted to be the anchor in the relay team against Lincoln, and he needed to show Coach Curry that he deserved it.

"Marko is training like his life depends on it," Trevor told Kevin. "He wants to knock you off your pedestal bro. A lotta pretty girls showing up for the practice runs, and he's playing to them too. He really likes Carissa. He's asked her out already, but she blew him off. It really burned him. When Carissa told him she loved to watch Twister run, he almost had a heart attack!"

At the final practice session before the meet against Lincoln, both Marko and Kevin did the 100-meter dash. Marko did it in 13 seconds and Kevin took 11 seconds. Immediately after the dash, Marko rushed to Coach Curry. "I don't know if you saw it or not, coach," Marko explained, "but the wind changed just before I started out. It was like one of those dust devils. It just screwed up my time."

Curry made some notes on his clip-board paper. Then the practice relay race got underway. This time Marko Lane was the anchor. Marko's face lit up with excitement. Starting the relay was Trevor, with Kevin doing the second lap, and a boy named Stacy Wong the third. Matson had asked to be left out of the relay that day.

Trevor started out strong, running his lap in excellent time, and smoothly passing the baton to Kevin. Once again Kevin lit up the course, putting the team in line for a record time before passing the baton to Stacy. Stacy was slower, but the team still had a chance for record time by the time Stacy passed the baton to Marko.

Now it all depended on Marko Lane. If he performed beyond anything he'd done before, the relay team would beat all its previous times.

Marko was running madly in the anchor lap, an almost frantic look on his face. His stride wasn't as smooth as usual. He was gasping when he crossed the finish line.

Coach Curry called out the time. "Four seconds short of our last effort."

"Wong slowed us down a lot," Marko said. "Did you see that Coach? If Wong had been a little faster, we would have made a new record." Marko turned to Wong and snapped, "You hurt us bad, Wong. You were really slow. You made the whole team look bad."

"Stick it in your ear, Lane," Wong came back at him. "You looked terrible in the anchor lap man. You looked like a puppet with broken strings."

Coach Curry stepped up. "Now look. I won't stand for this?" he stated firmly. "I won't play the blame game, and my team isn't going to play it either. Marko, I'll level with you. You have very poor sportsmanship. If a team member doesn't perform up to par, I will tell them in a polite and respectful way. I won't have you yelling at the guys and abusing them? If you don't think you can grasp what team spirit is, then you might want to get off the team. I want a united team against Lincoln. They're strong and they're not backbiters and whiners."

Coach Curry promised to announce the schedule for the meet the following afternoon. Everybody would be assigned their events and their positions in the relay. When Curry left the field, some of the Tubman students came up to talk to the track team.

"Twister, your lap was awesome," Carissa said.

Marko glanced over. "Just wait for the meet against Lincoln, baby. I have a feeling I'll be anchor and I'll win it for Tubman," he assured her.

Carissa smiled. "If I was Curry, I'd make Twister the anchor. That Lincoln team is really strong, and Twister has magic in his legs. But really all I want is for Tubman to win, no matter who runs in which lap."

"Yeah," Trevor said. "That's how we gotta look at it. How I do, or how Kevin does, or how Marko does, or how anybody does is only important for how the team does. I remember seeing a great football player on TV. He got three touchdowns in a game, but his team lost. They asked him if he was happy, and he said he's happy when the team wins, period."

"Way to go, Trev," Alonee exclaimed.

Marko came closer to Carissa. "I heard a rumor that you liked that new rap group— Mo-Pain. A little bird told me you got their stuff on your phone," he said.

"Yeah, I'm crazy about them," Carissa told him.

"They're coming to the Arena next week. Do you know about that?" Marko asked Carissa.

"Sure I know," Carissa said, "but nobody can get tickets, and, even if they could, they cost an arm and leg."

"I can get tickets," Marko said.

"Get outta here," Carissa protested. "They've been sold out for weeks!"

"I got tickets, babe. For you and me," Marko said with a grin.

"Marko Lane, you are putting me on," Carissa cried. Then she screamed. "For real? You can get me into the Mo-Pain concert?"

Marko grinned wider. "You got it, babe."

Carissa threw her arms around Marko's neck and yelled, "I'm going to see Mo-Pain, you guys! It's only the biggest concert to hit town this year!"

Marko and Carissa walked off together. Alonee turned to Trevor and said what they both knew. "His father will buy him anything he wants. Even hundreds of dollars for tickets. He'll put out a fortune so Marko can bribe some girl he wants into going with him."

"Hey Carissa," Sami called after her. "You ever date an octopus before, girl?"

Carissa turned, laughing. "A *what*?"

"He be all over you girl, like poison ivy," Sami hollered.

"She's all bent out of shape 'cause I would never date her," Marko said.

"Lot of stuff I never have had and won't miss," Sami said to the others. "Like an infected tooth, chicken pox, and a date with Marko Lane."

Sami, Trevor, Kevin, and Alonee shared a laugh. Then Sami said, "Matson Malloy has been really running. He's practicing all the time. He wants to win the two hundred meters against Lincoln. You know, it could happen. The Lincoln guys aren't strong in the two hundred meters. It'd be great if Matson won. It would raise him way, way up."

"I saw you and Matson at the movies, Saturday," Alonee said to Sami. "You guys were laughing up a storm, and it was a horror movie. You seem pretty happy."

Sami giggled. "That boy is a lot of fun. He been kicked around for a good long time, but now he coming out of his shell. He's shy, but when he opens up he can make you laugh till your stomach hurts," Sami said.

Kevin had seen Matson doing jumping jacks and stretching. He was running and practicing passing the baton too. Kevin hoped he'd be in the relay and win the 200-meter race. He deserved it.

On the following afternoon, the team gathered for Coach Curry's announcement. When he got to the relay race, he paused. "Now everybody, listen carefully. If there is any ill will about what I've decided, then get off the schedule right now. I don't want you competing in this meet. I won't have any spite going on in the relay. Winning depends on cooperation. I want four boys on that team who want Tubman to win a lot more than they want to show their own stuff. Am I clear?"

There was no sound from the track team. They shifted around nervously, but nobody said a word.

"Okay," Coach Curry went on. "In the relay team, the first lap will be run by Matson Malloy, and the second by Marko Lane. Trevor Jenkins will run the third, and Kevin Walker will anchor the team. That's where we're at. Any questions?"

Kevin glanced at Marko. He looked enraged but he forced a smile to his face. To Kevin it looked more like a grimace, but it satisfied the coach. As the team broke up to head home, Kevin spotted Marko following Matson. Marko was walking behind Matson silently for a few feet, then looked around to see if anyone was watching. He didn't see Kevin, who had ducked behind a line of trees on the edge of the campus.

"Listen freak," Marko hissed softly, "you screw me up at the meet Tuesday, and

I'll mess you up bad. Last time you almost dropped the baton and made a fool of me. It ain't happening again, freak, you hear what I'm saying?"

"I've been practicing the baton passing," Matson said. "I'm much better at it now. I can do it good now."

"Just remember, you ruin Tuesday for me, and you'll be sorry you were ever born," Marko warned.

Kevin stepped out from behind the row of eucalyptus trees. "Maybe I should tell Coach what I just heard," Kevin suggested. "Maybe you don't belong on the team, Marko."

Marko looked shocked and then a little frightened. "Hey dude, don't take everything so serious. Me and Matson were just joking, just horsing around, weren't we Matson? We're good buddies, right Matson?" Marko gave the other boy a playful shove.

Matson just stood there, then he stammered, "Yeah, we were joking around." All through Matson's life, he played along to get by, to survive. When child protective services first came to his home, he backed up his parents' claims that he got all his bruises by being clumsy. Matson knew in his heart that, if he was taken out of his parents' home, it would even be worse for him, and that was what happened. Now he could see no hope in turning Marko even more against him. So he smiled a shaky smile and said, "We're okay, me and Marko. Gonna be good on Tuesday. I'm much better than I was before. Gonna win the two-hundred-meter and then do us all proud in the relay. Go Tubman."

Marko threw his arm around Matson's shoulders and said, "You bet, Matson, we'll all be great." Marko was putting on a phony show of spirit and friendship because he was afraid of Kevin's ratting him out. Deep in Marko's heart he hated Kevin more than ever, but he smiled at Kevin and cheered, "Go Twister!"

The track meet was held on the Lincoln campus, but many Tubman students came.

Trevor brought Alonee, and Sami's father pulled up in a van loaded with kids. Great excitement was in the air. Such anticipation had never been felt before because everybody had always expected Tubman to lose. It had always been just a matter of how badly they would be beaten. Now the whiff of a possible win was in the air. Tubman usually looked good in the 100 and 200 meters. So now it looked like the relay race was there for the taking.

"It's you, Twister," Jaris Spain said. "You put the juice in the program."

Kevin was glad to be doing something good for Tubman, but he was nervous too. So much depended on him. He didn't want to let his school down.

CHAPTER SIX

Kevin Walker's first event on Tuesday was the 100 meters. He saw all the friendly Tubman faces wishing him well. Marko Lane was watching him too. Marko did not care if Kevin racked up points for Tubman High. Marko just wanted to do better than Kevin.

Kevin had broken speed records in this event back in Spurville, and he felt confident as he left the blocks. The boy from Lincoln jumped into the lead early. He had a magnificent effortless stride. Kevin had never run against such an obviously talented competitor. As they neared the halfway mark, Kevin surged forward, really flying toward the end, leaving the Lincoln boy two yards back.

A wild cheer went up from the stands where the Tubman fans sat. Kevin had beaten his own time, finishing the race in 10.5 seconds. Quickly though, the Lincoln track team moved ahead in points with some stellar performances, especially in the pole vault. When it was time for the relay race, the two teams were tied for points. The winner of the relay would win the meet.

Matson Malloy looked like someone going to his own execution as he got ready. It chilled Kevin to the bone to see the desperation on the boy's face. No doubt Marko's ugly words were replaying in his brain. Kevin was almost sorry that Matson was in the relay. No matter how much he had practiced, the emotional baggage from Marko's threats had to have undermined all his efforts.

Suddenly Matson was off, charging from the blocks, his arms pumping up and down. He looked good. He was breathing right. In the first lap Matson made superb time, but Marko waited to receive the baton—and that prospect had to send terror into Matson's soul. Still, the moment of the passing of the baton was so smooth and quick that it was scarcely visible. Kevin drew a sigh of relief as Marko sprinted through the second lap, doing well. At this point, the Tubman Titans' time was tied with the Lincoln team's. Marko successfully passed the baton to Trevor, and Trevor ran well, passing the baton with ease to Kevin for the anchor run.

Once more, the win depended on Kevin. He sprinted into overdrive, never looking back. When he sailed over the finish line, he was 2 seconds ahead of the Lincoln sprinter. Kevin had led the Titans to their first track meet victory in anybody's memory.

Coach Curry rushed to high-five and embrace his athletes. He told them all they had been awesome. The Tubman fans were going crazy in the stands. The chant went up, "Twist-er! Twist-er! Tubman Titans rule!"

From the corner of his eye, Kevin saw a girl leave the stands and come racing toward him. Carissa Polson flew into Kevin's arms, screaming, "You were amazing! You're wonderful, Twister!" Kevin smiled at the girl but he was surprised. He thought Marko's tickets to the Mo-Pain concert had put her in his camp.

Carissa stood on tiptoe and planted a wet kiss on Kevin's cheek. "My hero!" she sang out. "Everybody's hero!"

Marko had finished second in his best race, and now he stared at Carissa making a big deal over Kevin. "Hey babe," he called out, "I thought we were tight."

"Oh Marko, I'm sorry. I shoulda told you. I'm not going to the Mo-Pain concert after all. I'm sorry, but something else came up," Carissa said.

Marko turned to the boy closest to him, Trevor, and snarled, "That little witch. Playing a guy like a fool. I don't need a chick like her. I got my pick. There are ten girls who'd love to come to the concert with me, prettier girls than her too, the little piece of trash."

Trevor shrugged and said nothing. He didn't know much about Carissa. She had come to Tubman in her sophomore year, and she seemed a little boy crazy. She was cute and outgoing, the kind of girl Trevor never thought he had a chance with.

Carissa linked her arm with Kevin's and said, "Let's go celebrate at the Shrimp House, Twister. It's right down the street. My friend's boyfriend is a senior, and he's got a car."

Kevin climbed in the red convertible with Carissa, and they drove down the busy street to a seafood restaurant. The driver— the senior, Tony—yelled back at Kevin, "We're treating you, Kev. You won the day for Tubman today!"

Kevin's head was spinning. Nothing quite like this had ever happened to him before. And he never had a girl as beautiful as Carissa laying her head on his shoulder. He felt strange. He felt giddy, like when he ran and those endorphins were really kicking in.

"Why aren't you going to the Mo-Pain concert, Carissa?" Kevin asked her as they road in the car.

"I just changed my mind," Carissa told him. "Some girls told me Marko isn't nice on dates, and I didn't want a hassle after the concert."

They went into the restaurant, and a spread of shrimp came on a huge plate— Mediterranean grilled, garlic cream, and garlic herb. Kevin had never seen anything quite like it.

"Oh Kevin, you looked so cute running out there today in that tight shirt with your muscles bulging and those cute shorts. You were . . . awesome," Carissa cooed.

Kevin flushed. He concentrated on his shrimp.

Tony looked at Kevin and said, "You gotta watch out for Carissa. She gets carried away real easy. She's nuts about guys, and she doesn't judge too good. That's why she was going with that Lane dude. He's one gross dude. And another thing, Kevin, you want to introduce this girl to some good music, some nice cool jazz or something. Mo-Pain is nothing but a group of trash-talking rappers out to make money on being baaad."

"Tony is worse than my father," Carissa giggled.

"Getting real," Tony explained and turned to Kevin. "Everybody at Tubman is proud of you, Kevin. You've put us on the map. We have had a pathetic football team for a long time, and don't even talk about baseball. Only thing that wasn't totally lame was track, and you've lifted it from okay to great. You are the man dude."

"Thanks," Kevin responded, "but everybody is getting better." He was enjoying the company and enjoying the shrimp. He was especially enjoying Carissa. He had some girlfriends in Spurville, but he never

100

felt attracted to any of them. They were nice to be with, but they didn't make him feel like Carissa did. When Carissa snuggled close to Kevin, he had feelings he never had before. Carissa's hair smelled good, and she was wearing some perfume that made Kevin dizzy, but when she looked at him with those big brown eyes he got goose bumps.

When Kevin went home that day, he told his grandparents about the meet. "It was really good. That little guy I was worried about—Matson Malloy—he did really well in the two hundred meters. He almost won, and then he helped us win the relay. I won the hundred meters, and I anchored the relay, and Tubman got enough points to take the meet from Lincoln. Coach Curry was so happy. And then this girl—Carissa . . ."

Grandpa put down his crossword puzzle to listen.

"Carissa . . . that sure is a lovely sounding name," Grandma remarked.

"I'm telling you, Carissa acts like I'm some big TV star or something," Kevin went on. "I mean, she likes me a lot. You should've seen her when we won the meet. She comes running from the stands and flies into my arms, almost knocks me over. Then we all went to this ritzy place and had all kinds of shrimp and they treated me. It was all sorta amazing."

"Child, I ain't never seen you so happy in a long time, and it does my heart good," Grandma said, her face wreathed in smiles. "I know you been through a lot in this last year, and there've been nights I didn't sleep much worrying if you'd weather the storm, but now I got a lot of hope. I know your mama is watching from a better place, and she's pulling for you baby. My land, what a day you had! What a bountiful day!"

From the first time he saw Carissa, Kevin wanted to know her better. He never thought he had much of a chance with a girl like her, especially after Marko Lane waved those Mo-Pain tickets under her nose. Now, suddenly, she was laying her soft little head on his shoulder and making him dizzy with excitement.

The following Sunday, Kevin and Carissa took the city bus down to the bay and went walking along the coastline.

"What was it like living in Spurville?" Carissa asked as they strolled. "I mean, were you bored out of your mind and stuff?"

"No, nobody had much, but nobody was really poor either. My grandparents had a house in Spurville before they moved to California. That's where my mom grew up. Then she got a scholarship to go to Houston and study nursing. My mom got married there, and I was born in Houston."

Kevin stopped himself at that point. He was so comfortable with Carissa that he was talking too much. Mom and Dad met in Houston, and Kevin was born there all right. The three of them lived in an apartment. Then Dad got into the fight and went to prison, and Mom moved home to Spurville with Kevin. Nobody in Spurville knew what happened with Dad. They just assumed Mom's marriage failed and she came home to her family. When, later on, Dad died in the prison riot, nobody knew about his death either. Mom returned briefly to Houston for Charlie Walker's burial, where she stood beside his parents and a few other friends. If the truth had been known in Spurville, some people there would have gossiped and Mom didn't want that.

When Kevin was about eight, Grandma and Grandpa gave their house to Mom in Spurville, and they moved out to California to care for a sick relative. But every year, either they went home to Spurville or Mom came to California, and the family had a wonderful time together. Grandma cared for her sick sister and then her brother-in-law until they both died. And last year Kevin's grandparents went back to Spurville to be with their daughter until her time came.

"Houston is a great big city," Carissa said when Kevin fell silent. "I went through there once on a vacation. We came to all these skyscrapers, and I thought, wow, what a city, and then Mom said, 'Oh no, we're not in Houston yet. This is just the outskirts!' And then we got to Houston, and, whoa, I didn't know the city was so big! Wow, I bet it was hard leaving Houston for little Spurville, huh?"

"I was only three. I don't remember much," Kevin replied.

"Your mom's a nurse, huh?" Clarissa asked, and then went on. "I bet she misses you out here living with your grandparents. I mean, I'm sure glad she sent you because we all love you so much, but I bet your mom misses you."

Kevin had given the idea to everyone that he left his family in Spurville to live with his grandparents for the better educational opportunities. His parents supposedly wanted something better for him. Kevin didn't want to admit to being an orphan for fear of all the sympathy he would get and did not want.

But Kevin felt so close to Carissa that he broke his own rule. "Carissa, I haven't told anybody this, and I need for you to keep it just between us. I didn't want people pitying me or feeling sad for me. You see, my mom died a few months ago," Kevin revealed.

An instant look of sadness came over Carissa's face. "Oh Kevin! *I'm so sorry*. You've been carrying all that pain in your heart *alone*!" she cried.

"Carissa, please, don't do that," Kevin insisted. "I'm coping with it. It still hurts a lot, but it hurts more when people get all emotional. Then I fall to pieces too. Mom raised me strong. I'm okay. I feel close to you, Carissa, so that's why I told you, but don't tell anybody."

"I won't, I promise, Kevin," Carissa swore. "But what about your dad?"

"Oh, he died a long time ago. It was just me and Mom against the world. I hardly knew my dad," Kevin explained.

"Kevin," Carissa said, her voice thick with emotion, "I just want you to know that

I respect you even more for having gone through so much, and still coming here and having so much school spirit and caring for people. I just think you're beautiful, inside and out."

"Carissa," Kevin responded, "I'm just a guy. I'm doing my best. Most people are. We all have to deal with stuff."

"Kevin," Carissa said in a small voice, "I don't want to make you feel bad or anything, but do you have her picture? Your mom's?"

"Yeah, sure, I look at it all the time," Kevin said, digging it out of his wallet and showing it to Carissa.

"Oh Kevin, she's beautiful. You look like her, especially your eyes," Carissa remarked.

"Yeah, everybody said that," Kevin said, closing the wallet. "Now let's go watch the seagulls. Hear them screaming out there?"

They continued walking as the seagulls filled the air. Pelicans were joining them.

"I always liked the pelicans," Kevin commented. "They look so funny. I read a poem on a postcard once: "A wonderful bird is the pelican, its beak can hold more than its bellican.' "

"Yeah," Carissa laughed, "they dive down and scoop everything up and then drain off what isn't food. Some of the fishermen don't like them because they take so many fish."

"Like Mr. Buckingham's been telling us, we've got to coexist with the wild things. We can't hog the whole earth and all that's here," Kevin said. "My grandparents go to the local church. Pastor Bromley, he gave a good talk the other Sunday. He said, yeah, God gave man dominion over the earth and all its creatures, but He didn't give us the right to destroy everything."

Kevin and Carissa got ice cream cones at a little beach stand, then turned around for the walk back to the bus stop. It was one of the best days Kevin had had in a long time.

As he headed to his grandparents house after leaving Carissa, Kevin still felt a little uneasy about sharing his mother's death with Carissa. He didn't want his personal life known around school. It wasn't so much that he didn't want anybody to know that his mother had died, but he was just nervous that more questions would follow and those were the ones he didn't want to deal with.

Mom told Kevin when he was about seven that, if anybody asks about his father, he just should say, "My dad died a long time ago, and I don't remember him much." Mom told Kevin that he did not need to be ashamed of his father. Nothing that had happened was Kevin's fault. But it was best that people did not know about the arrest, the conviction, and the death in the prison riot. "Some people, if they knew all that, would try to use it to hurt you," Mom explained.

The truth of his mother's words came to Kevin as Buck Sanders mercilessly taunted him without even knowing about Charlie

Walker. Kevin could only imagine what it would have been like had Buck known that Kevin was the son of a convicted murderer. Now Kevin could imagine what Marko Lane would do with such information. Marko was looking for a way to undermine Kevin. This would be a gift on a silver platter, a way to raise doubt in the minds of some of the Tubman students. This Kevin Walker, *who was he really*? How far does the apple fall from the tree? Can a boy ever completely escape the shadow of such a father?

"Did you have a nice time with Carissa?" Grandma asked.

"Yeah, we just watched the birds and walked and talked," Kevin said.

"Yes," Grandma remarked, "we need people to talk to. All kinds of people, some our own age. In many ways, only somebody your age can understand you."

CHAPTER SEVEN

Tubman High School put on a spring school dance every year, and Kevin asked Carissa right away. "I didn't want somebody else to beat me to it," he admitted, grinning. He was smiling a lot more these days.

"Like I would've gone with anybody else," Carissa chided. "If you hadn't asked me, I woulda asked *you*. Sami said there's no reason a girl can't do the asking. It's a whole new world out there. Yeehah!"

The theme of the dance was Green Glory, a tip of the hat to the local flora that didn't require a lot of water. The school auditorium was going to be decorated with flowering ice plant, cactus, and different succulents.

Some of the parents volunteered to help with the dance, including Alonee's parents, Sami's parents, and Trevor's mother.

"Maybe you should get your grandparents to come and help, Kevin," Marko said snidely. "Only they're so old they'd have to come in their wheelchairs." Marko laughed and his friends joined in dutifully.

Kevin gave Marko and his friends a dirty look and continued helping Alonee compile the list of parent volunteers.

"When are your grandparents gonna go to the nursing home, Kevin?" Marko persisted. "I seen your grandfather the other day, stumbling around the front yard, and he looked confused like he has Alzheimer's or something."

"You know, Lane," Kevin said, "why don't you mind your own business? We're trying to get this dance organized, and all you're doing is standing around making stupid comments."

Marko laughed. "Don't be so touchy. I guess guys from Texas have shorter tempers.

It comes from being around nasty steers so much. I guess the fragrance of cow manure gets into your attitude," he nagged.

"Yeah," Tyron Becker joined in, "Texan dudes are mean and ornery, Marko. Don't get Walker mad, or he might pull out a big Bowie knife and slice us up."

"I don't carry a knife," Kevin snapped. "If you guys weren't so stupid, you'd know it's against school rules to carry weapons."

"Tyron, he's calling us stupid," Marko said. "He's got a baaad attitude."

"Mom's gonna make sure we got good stuff to snack on," Sami remarked. Sami's mother had volunteered to organize the refreshments.

"I bet she does that real good," Marko told her. "She's sure got you stuffed with enough food to feed a herd of hippos."

Kevin turned sharply. "Lane," he asked directly, "instead of standing there making freakin' comments, why don't you ask your parents to help with this dance? I'd sure like to meet your parents. I'd like to meet the kind of people who raised a son without manners or compassion. I'd like to ask them what they think went wrong."

The smile left Marko's face. "I got great parents," he snarled. "You should talk, Walker. You got a mother living in Texas who shipped you out here to live with a doddering old couple. That's how much your mother cares about you."

Carissa looked at Kevin. Her eyes asked the question, "Why don't you tell him the truth? Why do you let him go on believing you've got a mother who has chosen not to be with her son?" Kevin thought to himself that he didn't owe anybody any explanations. Then he noticed the uneasy expressions on the faces of his friends.

Nobody came right out and asked Kevin why he was out here with just his grandparents, but Alonee and Jaris looked puzzled. Why would the mother of such a wonderful son not want to be with him? Why would a mother not want to share in the life of such a wonderful son?

Kevin took a deep breath, then faced them all. "When I came here from Texas, I didn't know anybody. I just wanted to be left alone. I didn't want to talk about my life. I thought, if people knew the whole story, I'd get a lot of attention I couldn't handle. So I just made it easy for myself. I said my folks sent me to live with my grandparents because the schools out here are better than we got in Spurville. I should have been up front in the beginning."

They were all looking at him. There was a deep silence, almost a hush. Kevin spoke briskly. "My parents are dead. My dad died when I was very small, and my mom died a few months ago. I came here to live with my grandparents because they are the only family I have. So now you know, and that's the end of it. Don't anybody tell me how sorry they are. If you're one of my friends, then I *know* you're sorry and that's all I need to know. If you're not one of my friends, then you don't care and that's okay too. Don't anybody make a big deal of it. Let's just finish this list of parent volunteers."

Everybody got quietly back to the business at hand, but the atmosphere was different. Even Marko decided not to say anything until Kevin and Carissa were almost done walking out the door. Then Kevin overheard Marko say, "I don't believe what that dude told us. He just made that up. He's got some deep, dark secrets from Spurville, and he made up that sob story. He's afraid we'll find out who he really is."

"Maybe there was a crime down there," Tyron said. "Maybe like his parents were big criminals, drug dealers or something. You hear about stuff like that all the time. Kevin is a creepy guy. He's got some skeletons in his closet, that's for sure."

Kevin's hands involuntarily hardened into fists. He wanted to grab Marko and Tyron and bang their heads together. He could almost hear the knock of their skulls echo off the gymnasium walls, and he could almost see them drop unconscious to the floor.

Carissa put her hand over Kevin's. "Just ignore them," she urged. "They're not worth it. Let's just pretend we didn't even hear them. Everybody knows what they are. They just want to hurt people."

Kevin and Marko both continued to improve on the track team as they prepared for the next meet against El Capitan. They were both running in the 100-meter race, and Marko was determined to win this time. Marko wasn't sure he could win against a Kevin Walker at his best, but he hoped he might unearth something in Kevin's path to throw him off his stride.

Grandpa Roy Stevens was out working his vegetable garden one day, when Tyron Becker came along. Grandpa already knew Marko Lane as a troublemaker, but he didn't know Tyron.

"Looks like you're putting in your tomatoes, eh sir?" Tyron asked in a respectful tone. He thought a man of old age would appreciate respect from a boy.

"Yep. Always been proud of my tomatoes. I don't like to brag, but folks tell me they're tastier than anything you can get in a store," Grandpa said.

"I go to Tubman High," Tyron told him. "Your grandson is well liked there. He's a fine athlete."

The old man grinned proudly. "Well, that's nice to hear. We sure are proud of him. His mama called him Twister 'cause he's always been quick as a Texas tornado. You a friend of Kevin's?" he asked.

"Yeah," Tyron lied.

"What's your name boy?" Grandpa Roy asked. He had a pretty good memory, and he was familiar with most of the names Kevin mentioned as his friends.

"Uh . . . Bill," Tyron finally answered. "We just got to be friends. He probably hasn't said much about me. I think it's great that you guys are making a home for Kevin, him being an orphan and all. That's rough."

"Well, the boy is a pleasure to have around. He lights up our old age. Gives us a reason for going on I guess. When you get to be almost eighty you're apt to want to sit in your rocking chair, but the boy livens things up," Grandpa said.

"It's really awful what happened to Kevin's parents down there in Spurville," Tyron remarked, moving into his fishing expedition. He wanted to trick the old man into thinking he already knew some terrible truth. Tyron figured that, at his age, the old man could be easily tricked into revealing the whole story.

"Well," Grandpa said vaguely, "we don't understand why these things happen to good folks. We just got to trust in the Lord that He knows what He's doing and it'll all turn out right in the end."

"Yeah, but it must have been a big shock when it happened," Tyron said.

Grandpa Roy carefully planted the tomato deep in the ground. That was the secret of his good tomatoes. Put the plant down deep enough. He tamped the good black earth around it. Then he looked up at the boy. "Say what?" he asked.

"I was just thinking it must have been horrible when the thing happened like that, I mean, when your lives were like shattered by the . . . you know." Tyron stumbled over his words, trying desperately to lure the old man into revealing something. Tyron valued his friendship with Marko. It meant going to places you couldn't afford on your own. Marko's father had deep pockets, and Tyron benefited too. He had to bring Marko something—something he could use against Kevin.

"We were expecting our daughter to pass on," Grandpa Roy said. "It just about broke our hearts. Our daughter was our only child. When she got sick, we had a lot of hope and the doctors tried hard, but it was not to be. We had to let her go into the Lord's hands."

Tyron was worried now. Maybe there was no deep, terrible secret. "Your son-in-law was already dead then?" he asked. "How did he die?"

Grandpa Roy planted another tomato deep. He tamped the earth. He got slowly to his feet and brushed the dirt from the knees of his overalls. He straightened his arthritis-crippled body a little. "You ask a lot of questions boy," he stated sternly.

"Yeah," Tyron said nervously. "I like Kevin and I'm real interested in his . . . uh . . . life, you know?"

The old man's eyes narrowed. "Boy, the more I look at you, the more I don't like the looks of you. You got eyes like a snake I once found hiding under the chicken coop. He was looking to eat my chicks. What are you after?" Grandpa Roy demanded.

Tyron gave up on the first plan, soft-soaping the old man in the hopes he'd release the information. Now Tyron turned to Plan B. "There's something awful in Kevin's past, isn't there? We don't know all the details, but we're pretty sure he's hiding something real ugly and some of the kids at

121

Tubman are afraid of him. You better tell me the truth, mister, 'cause some of the kids want to run him outta school."

"You git your hide off my property boy. I got me a shotgun, and, if you ain't long gone before I have time to git it, you're gonna be picking buckshot out of your behind for a good long time. So git!" Grandpa Roy commanded.

Tyron hurried off the property and jogged down the street away from the house on Iroquois Street. He had nothing promising to tell Marko, but the old man did seem pretty riled up, as if there were a secret of some kind. If there were nothing to it at all, would he have gotten so angry?

Roy Stevens went into the house and told Lena about the boy. "He was up to no good," he concluded.

"It wasn't that Marko Lane was it?" Grandma asked.

"No, I know that skunk by the sight of him," Grandpa said.

When Kevin got home from school, Grandpa told him about the visitor.

"I bet it was Tyron Becker," Kevin guessed. "He does Marko's dirty work for him. Was he kinda flabby in the middle?"

"Yep, that he was," Grandpa Roy affirmed. "A lazy-looking boy. I told him to git if he didn't want his rear end filled with buckshot."

Kevin grinned at his grandfather. Right now, with his eyes on fire, Grandpa Roy didn't look almost eighty. He looked like he must have looked years ago when he came courting Lena Grady or when he fought in the Battle of Chosin Reservoir in Korea and earned a medal for valor.

During track practice on Wednesday afternoon, Coach Curry pitted his four fastest boys against each other in the 100-meter trial run. Trevor, Marko, Matson, and Kevin all ran. Sami stood on the sidelines wearing a T-shirt that read, "Go Matson #1." She and Matson had become inseparable, and

Matson was basking in the glow of having a first girlfriend—and someone who really believed in him. Kevin thought that the way Matson had been training, there was a chance he'd win the race.

The four boys waited for the signal and then charged out of the blocks. Matson took the lead at once, followed by Marko. Kevin was third, and Trevor brought up the rear. Once again Marko was so frantic to win that he was tight. Everything about him was tense and unnatural. His arms weren't swinging at his sides as they should have been. Instead, he made fists of his hands as he ran.

Trevor overtook him, leaving Kevin and Matson running side by side. They were setting a torrid pace. Matson slipped over the finish line a second before Kevin.

Both Kevin and Matson embraced at the end of the race. "Matson, you were awesome," Kevin cried. "You've improved so much I can't believe it. You were greased lightning!"

Matson grinned happily. "You go, Twister," he said.

Trevor passed Marko, who came in last in a wretched performance, stumbling over the finish line like a drunken man. His face was transfixed with rage. It was not about running anymore. He had to beat Kevin. He had to. When Carissa flew into Kevin's arms and Alonee was hugging Trevor, Sami clutched Matson. Marko turned his back on all of them, hurrying off the field. Coach Curry followed him. "Marko, we all have bad days. You're a much better runner than you just showed. Don't let it get you down," he said. Marko ignored him, quickening his pace off the field.

Kevin was getting to like Carissa more with each passing day. He enjoyed being with her no matter what they did. Just stopping for a burrito with her was a big deal. Kevin was usually a quiet person, but he wanted to pour out his heart and his dreams to Carissa.

One evening, Kevin and Carissa walked down to a little pizza place and sat there talking.

"I had my first boyfriend when I was fourteen," Carissa said. "I was really stupid. He was like sixteen. My mom, you know, I love her so much, but she wants to be my pal. We're more like girlfriends than mother and daughter. She's really young. She never wants to boss me around, you know. My dad, he's even worse. He acts really young. He loves my music. He calls me "Daddy's little girl," but he doesn't, you know, protect me . . ."

Carissa looked sad for a moment. Then she went on. "This guy I dated . . . he took me to the beach one night. Big party going on. What did I know? I was fourteen. Everybody drinking beer and smoking dope too. I didn't even know what those pills were. I mean, I drink wine at my house, but they were chug-a-lugging beer and some whisky too . . . I never drank so much like that night . . ."

Kevin felt sorry for Carissa. He sensed where this was going. Her parents shouldn't have let her date a sixteen-year-old. They shouldn't have let her go to an all-night beach party. But they did.

"I was so drunk . . ." Carissa continued, "I didn't know what was happening. Some people called the cops from a house. The cops took me to the hospital for alcohol poisoning. I was so ashamed. I shouldn't even be telling you this, Kevin. You'll think I'm a bad person . . ."

CHAPTER EIGHT

I don't think you're a bad person, Carissa," Kevin assured her.

"Well, my parents didn't get mad at me or anything," she went on. "They took me home and said all kids do stupid stuff, but, you know, I was going to a different school then and my reputation got really trashed. Those boys at the beach party told horrible stories about me, and I was so drunk I didn't even know what all happened. I felt like a rotten person, Kevin. Oh Kevin, I bet now you think I'm some trashy girl!" Carissa groaned.

"Carissa, you're not. You were just a kid. Your parents sorta failed you. A fourteen-year-old girl with sixteen-year-old guys!

That's just asking for big trouble," Kevin told her. He felt sorry for Carissa. She was probably sorry she had said anything at all about that beach party.

Clarissa explained how she felt. "Kevin, you're such a good person, and your grandparents are nice churchgoing people. I bet your mom was good as gold too. I don't know why I said so much. I mean, I've never told any of this to anybody at this school. I just care about you so much, and I thought would you like me if you knew what a stupid thing I'd done? I just knew if I told you, I'd be safe because you'd never tell anybody else."

Kevin wanted desperately to put Carissa at ease. So he did something he thought he would never do. He decided to share his secret too. "Carissa, there are problems in every family. My own father was in prison . . . he died in prison." Kevin blurted it out.

Carissa stared at Kevin. "Oh Kevin, that must have been so hard," she said.

Kevin told Clarissa about his secret. "I was just a little kid when it all happened, but it was tough on Mom. Dad got in a fight with another guy, and the guy cracked his head on the concrete curb and died. So my father went up for second-degree murder. I was just three years old. All I knew was that Dad didn't take me to the park anymore and buy me strawberry ice cream. And then there was a riot at the prison, and some guards got hurt and some prisoners got killed. One of them was my father. I was about six. I had sort of forgotten my dad by then. I hadn't seen him in such a long time. But they gave Mom his body, and she went to his funeral in Houston. She left me with my grandparents."

Carissa reached over and covered Kevin's hands with her own. "Kevin, that is so sad."

Kevin dug the picture of his father from his wallet and showed it to Carissa. "He was about twenty here," he explained.

"Oh, he was so handsome, Kevin," Carissa remarked. "I bet that deep down he was a nice man who just made some dumb decisions that got him in trouble. Like me going to that stupid party. That's what's so awful about life. You make mistakes, and sometimes you can't fix them because you don't get a second chance."

"My father was a boxer," Kevin said, "a really good one. He won a lot of fights as a lightweight. He was on his way to qualifying for the Olympics, but stuff happened. He always struggled with a bad temper. I got that too. I have to work at keeping it under control."

When they left the pizza place, they walked through a field where there were old pepper trees. A house used to stand on this lot, but it burned down years ago and all you could see were a few foundation stones and the pepper trees. Kevin and Carissa sat on the foundation stones and huddled in each other's arms. Kevin had never felt this close to anyone in his life outside his family. Kevin touched Carissa's cheek and turned her face toward him. He kissed her gently on the lips. She kissed him back, and, when they got up to walk on, their hands were linked.

After Carissa walked up the steps to the apartment where she lived, she stopped and waved to Kevin. Then he went on alone.

A strange, almost terrifying feeling came over Kevin as he neared home. He had told his secret. He had sworn to himself that he would never do that. But he had told Carissa because he was so eager to tell her something personal about himself when she shared her story of the beach party. His defenses had crumbled in his desire to comfort her.

Kevin told himself now that he had nothing to worry about. Carissa would never betray his secret. He had no doubt of that. And yet he felt vulnerable in a way he had not felt before. The bird had flown the cage. The door stood open. The bird was flying, who knew where?

Kevin did not tell his grandparents what he had done. He couldn't. He felt that in a way he had betrayed his agreement with them.

Tubman High School was decorated with real and papier-mâché cactus and ice-plant flowers. Trevor's mother was in charge of tickets, and Sami's mother was at the refreshment table. Everybody knew there would be no spiking of the punch with Sami's mother in charge.

Jaris Spain's mother was chatting with Alonee's mom as the couples started arriving. When Kevin came in with Carissa, he overheard Jaris's mother saying, "Oh dear, is that Nattie Harvey? She'll spend the whole evening gossiping about everybody. Her kids have all graduated already. I don't know why she comes to these events. I just hate seeing her."

Alonee's mother nodded. "One time I was yelling at one of my kids, and the next day everybody at church was offering to help me because obviously I was 'overstressed' and overwhelmed with being a mother. Nattie had heard me, and she wasted no time in spreading the word."

Jaris's mother chimed in. "She saw my husband one time unshaven and in his dirty work clothes, and before we knew it she was saying he lost his job and was now one of the street people. I was so embarrassed. I wish everybody would just stop talking to that woman."

Kevin glanced at Mrs. Harvey. She was a tall, mature looking woman with hard eyes. She was now in an animated conversation with two other women. As Mrs. Harvey talked, she seemed to be glancing over at Kevin. He was sure it was just his imagination and yet . . .

It had been two days since Kevin shared his secret with Carissa. He was still nervous about it.

"Carissa," Kevin asked, "am I imagining things, or is Mrs. Harvey looking my way a lot?"

Carissa shrugged. "I'm sure she's not interested in us. She's probably just looking around," she replied.

Kevin and Carissa danced as the DJ put on all the right songs, a mix of the top forty with some reggae thrown in. Marko had made a date with a pretty girl named Jasmine, and he made it a point to be in the middle of the dance floor with Jasmine so that everyone would see his conquest. It was not until late, when the evening was winding down, that Marko walked over to where Kevin and Carissa were.

"Hey Carissa," Marko said, "you doing okay?"

"Sure Marko, why not?" Carissa answered. "I'm having a wonderful time."

"You can't be too careful with guys, babe," Marko said. "We all grew up together around here, but Walker here came blowing in from Texas a few weeks ago and who knows about him." As he spoke, Marko's eyes seemed to bore into Kevin like lasers. He had a smirk on his lips that sent cold chills down Kevin's spine. Kevin couldn't escape the uneasy feeling that something was wrong.

"What's with you, Lane?" Kevin finally asked. "What stupid mind game you playing now?"

Marko continued to stare at Kevin; then he said softly, "You sweatin' a little, bro? I hope you're wearing good underarm protection, 'cause looks to me like you're sweatin'. Yeah. I can see sweat jumping out on your forehead man. Hey, that's too bad. You must be nervous about something. That's not going to help your running game at El Capitan, you hear what I'm saying?"

"Are you drunk or what?" Kevin snapped.

Marko shook his head. "I'm stone cold sober man," he sneered. "I'm being a good boy. No booze, no pills. Everything going along fine in my life. I got a great looking chick—Jasmine—who can't get enough of me. And I got no worries. You don't see me sweatin'—no way. But listen man, try not to let those worries get the best of you. When you lay down to sleep tonight, don't let them gnaw at you like bedbugs." He jammed his finger into Kevin's chest, "Don't let the bedbugs bite." Then Marko strolled off to find Jasmine.

"He's trying to mess with my mind," Kevin said to Carissa. "He can't win at El Capitan against me, so he hopes to mess me up mentally and get me off my stride."

"What a freak," Carissa commented with contempt.

But Kevin couldn't help wondering if there was more to Marko's behavior than just empty mind games. Did Marko know something? Had the secret about Kevin's father leaked? But how could it? Kevin told only Carissa, and she would never betray him. Kevin was willing to stake his life on that. Carissa wouldn't do anything to hurt Kevin. Still, there was something different about Marko, a kind of smug, self-confidence that he had not showed before. Marko had been angry, frustrated, and agitated in his eagerness to beat Kevin at the meet. Now, suddenly, he seemed to have an ace in the hole.

As he headed home, Kevin wondered if Grandpa had accidentally revealed the secret the other day when Tyron came around asking questions. Grandpa swore he didn't let anything slip in conversation, but sometimes Grandpa got a little mixed up about things. Lately he couldn't do his bank statements right, and Grandma had to take over, making sure he was deducting the amounts of the checks he wrote. A couple of checks had bounced. And Grandpa had finally agreed to stop driving his beloved pickup after he missed some stop signs.

Kevin didn't have the heart to question Grandpa about his conversation with Tyron. Instead, that night, Kevin remarked, "Grandpa, I'm sure glad you didn't fall for it when Marko's friend came around digging for information the other day."

Grandpa chuckled. "I seen enough snakes in my time to recognize one that comes slithering up boy," he said.

That night, Kevin had trouble falling asleep. Marko's evil prediction came true. Marko's sneering face kept looming before him. Marko's taunt rang in his ears. Kevin was tossing. He was changing positions. Suddenly, in the dark doorway of his room, he saw his grandmother. "You all right, Kevin? I hear you tossin' and turnin'. You giving those bedsprings a workout. You're not sick, are you?" Grandma asked.

"I'm okay, Grandma. It was an exciting evening, the dance and everything. And the meet at El Capitan is coming up. I'm just thinking about everything," Kevin told her. Though none of that answer was true, it satisfied Grandma. The truth was that Marko Lane had managed to get under Kevin's skin. Kevin was pretty sure Marko knew nothing, but he had a small, frightening fear that somehow Marko knew everything—that he knew Kevin's father had killed someone and that he died in a prison riot. Kevin could imagine the looks from fellow students if that became common knowledge. Everything at Tubman would change for Kevin. Carissa already knew, so she would stick by Kevin, but it just wouldn't be the same around school.

But how could Marko Lane have found out? How?

A large crowd came from Tubman to El Capitan for the meet on Friday. Kevin saw all his friends smiling and waving at him as he got ready for the event he had trained hard for: the 100-meter dash. Four boys from Tubman and four from El Capitan were running. The 100-meter was not a strong race for the El Capitan boys, so it looked like a Tubman Titan could win and take second place.

As Kevin waited for the race to begin, Marko came over. "Hey, you look tired man. Didn't you sleep good last night? That's too bad. Good athletes need their sleep, but then you got a lot on your mind," Marko commented, winking.

Kevin ignored him but felt tense. That feeling was uncommon for him before a race. He worried that his muscles were tightening up.

Marko leaned over and said barely above a whisper, "Hey Twister," he hissed. "What was your daddy's name? Was he named Kevin too? Like father, like son . . ."

At the signal, the eight runners took off, but Kevin knew something was wrong. He wasn't getting the speed he needed. His legs lacked the spring they always had. He wasn't even breathing right.

Marko Lane surged ahead and was neck in neck with Matson Malloy. A boy from El Capitan was closing in on them. Kevin was lagging, barely passing Trevor and two other boys from El Capitan. It turned out to be a slow 100-meter race with no new records. It was the worst 100 meters Kevin ever ran, and he wasn't even close when a boy from El Capitan beat Marko Lane over the finish line. Coach Curry came over to Kevin, concern on his face, "Kevin, you were way off your stride. Are you okay?" he asked.

"Yeah Coach, I'm sorry. I'm really tired. I feel kinda weak," Kevin explained.

"You need to see the doctor. Maybe you caught a bug," Curry said. "The boy who just ran that race in your lane wasn't you Kevin. Do you want to be pulled from the relay?"

"No, I can do it," Kevin insisted. "I can get myself together and do it." He was determined that the day would not turn out to be a complete rout for Tubman. He forced Marko Lane's ugly taunts from his mind by sheer force of will and tried to prepare himself to anchor the Tubman team.

Marko started the relay and ran a good lap, passing the baton to Trevor without a hitch. Trevor ran well, but not great, passing the baton to Matson, who ran a fine lap and smoothly gave the baton to Kevin. Tubman was narrowly ahead of El Capitan thanks to a good pole vault earlier, but Kevin knew losing the relay race would give the meet to El Capitan. The loss would be a bitter disappointment to the Tubman fans, who were expecting a great day.

The most inspirational person ever in his life was his mother. So Kevin brought her beautiful face into his mind as he ran. He remembered all her encouraging words throughout his life, even toward the end when she knew she wouldn't be around much longer. "You'll be great Twister. You'll make me proud! Even if I'm with the angels, I'll be cheering for you, Twister!"

When Kevin's fingers closed on the baton, he felt the old speed return to his legs. He was breathing well and his legs were flying. The cheers from the Tubman fans were all he needed to push him over the finish line a few seconds ahead of the El Capitan team. The familiar chants came from the stands: "Twist-er! Twist-er!"

Marko Lane stood on the sidelines looking dumbfounded. Marko's hopes had risen when Kevin lost the 100-meter race. He couldn't believe Kevin had recovered enough to run the anchor lap so well.

Kevin looked around for Carissa. Usually she would be racing from the stands screaming at this point. He hoped she wasn't so discouraged when he lost the 100-meter race that she ran off somewhere.

"Alonee," Kevin called out, "have you seen Carissa?"

"No," Alonee called back. "One minute she was right beside me and the next minute she was gone."

Another girl spoke up then. "She was crying really hard, Kevin. When you lost the 100-meter race, she just burst into tears and started running toward the parking lot. I tried to get her to come back, but that girl was like freakin'."

"That's weird," Kevin said. "She's gotta know that you can't win them all." Kevin never expected Carissa to act like this. He was surprised and a little worried. He knew Carissa was proud of his running ability, but why would she take it so hard when he lost one race? Kevin was sure their relationship was built on something stronger than the fact that he could run well.

Kevin walked all over the field looking for Carissa. He thought maybe she was sulking nearby. But then surely she would have heard the cheers go up when Kevin successfully anchored the relay race. Surely then she would have come back.

Carissa had planned to ride home with Trevor, his friends, and two seniors from Tubman. So Kevin went to the parking lot and found the van.

"You guys seen Carissa?" he asked Trevor.

"No, we been waiting for her to show up," Trevor told him, "but then somebody said they saw her running down to the bus stop. So I guess she caught a bus home."

Kevin rode back to their neighborhood with Trevor and the others, but he didn't go directly home. He jogged, alone, over to the apartment where Carissa lived. As he stood out front, he dialed her on her cell phone.

"Yeah?" came Carissa's voice. She sounded strange. Her voice was thick, as though she'd been crying.

"Carissa, this is Kevin. I helped the team win the relay, so Tubman won the day. Alonee said you ran off when I lost the 100 meters. I was really surprised that you'd take it so hard. You can't let stuff like that get to you," Kevin said.

Carissa didn't say anything.

"Carissa, listen. I want to talk to you. Come on down and we'll go somewhere for a cola or something. Or should I come up there?" Kevin asked.

"Kevin, I ca-can't talk to you now. Just go away. Please, just go away," Carissa responded in a halting voice.

"I'm not going away. Carissa, what's the matter with you? You got me really worried now. There's something wrong with you. I'm not leaving here until I find out what it is. You might as well not try to hide from me," Kevin insisted.

CHAPTER NINE

K evin," Carissa sobbed, "I did something horrible. I can't face you. If you knew what I did, you would hate me forever and I wouldn't blame you. I hate myself. I can't bear to see you, Kevin. Just go away and pretend I don't even exist!"

Kevin closed his cell phone. He walked to the apartment and went up the stairs to Apartment 2B, which he saw Carissa enter last week. He hit the doorbell and waited. In a few seconds a very pretty woman in her thirties, dressed like a teenager, opened up. She looked like a slightly older version of Carissa, so Kevin figured it was her mother. "Hi," he said. "I'm Kevin Walker. I need to see Carissa. She's a friend of mine from school."

"Come on in Kevin. Carissa has told me all about you. You're that amazing Twister! Poor Carissa is all upset right now and it's my bad. It's all my fault I'm afraid," Mrs. Polson said.

"What are you talking about? What happened?" Kevin asked.

"Well, Carissa and I are *very* close," Mrs. Polson explained. We talk about everything. She doesn't hide anything from me. Some kids don't tell their parents anything. Not Carissa. She's like my best girlfriend and vice versa. Anyway, Kevin, she really cares about you. She's never felt that way about a boy before. Well, she told me about your father."

"What?" Kevin asked, his mouth going dry. Carissa shared his secret with her mother?

"Oh Kevin," Carissa's mother went on, "she admires you so much, and all the more when she learned of your tragic background. To think you've made so much of your life overcoming all *that*. She said your father was in prison for killing a man and then he died there in a riot, but she didn't want any of the kids at school to know, because they might make it hard for you. Of course, I understood that. Kids can be so cruel about such things. Carissa feels so awful that somehow the story leaked out . . . she thinks she betrayed you and she's heartbroken. She is sure you can never forgive her."

"How could the story have leaked out?" Kevin asked.

"I don't know, but Carissa is sure it has. She said this nasty creature—Marko Lane—he knows about it and he's already taunting you. Carissa is just sure that it's all over Tubman and she feels so guilty." Mrs. Polson curled up in a leather chair and began applying fingernail polish as she talked.

"I want to see Carissa," Kevin said grimly.

"Well, that's her bedroom door at the end of the hall. Just go down there and knock. Good luck to you Kevin. You seem like such a wonderful boy. Poor Carissa is just devastated that she has hurt you," Mrs. Polson said.

Kevin rapped on Carissa's door. "Carissa, listen. I need to talk to you. Open the door," he urged.

"Kevin, I can't look at you!" Carissa almost screamed.

"Come on, just open the door. We'll talk. Don't be afraid. Carissa . . . just open the door. Your mom told me that you told her about my father. It's okay, Carissa. I'm not angry. Honest I'm not," Kevin said.

There was a moment's silence. Kevin heard her coming to the door. She drew the latch across. When she opened the door, Kevin reached out and took her in his arms. "It's okay, Carissa. You told me you and your mom are real tight. I shouldn't have told you something I didn't want to share with your mom. It's my fault," he said.

Carissa drew back, her eyes red from crying. "Don't you hate me, Kevin?" she asked in a shaky voice.

"No, I don't hate you girl. I could never hate you, Carissa. Don't be silly," Kevin said.

"But the story leaked out because of me," Carissa protested, beginning to cry again.

Kevin felt a little numb. He didn't have the whole story yet. "How could that have happened, Carissa?" he asked gently.

Carissa turned away from Kevin. She looked out the window. She saw her mother talking to the next-door neighbor. She was waving her hand in the air to hasten the drying of her red polish. "She's a gossip, Kevin," Carissa said in a tiny voice.

"Who is?" Kevin asked. He thought he probably knew the answer.

"Mom. She reads movie magazines all day and she gossips. She gossips about the people on TV and all the people she knows," Carissa explained.

"Carissa, if you know that, why did you tell her?" Kevin asked.

"I don't blame you for hating me. I hate myself. I could just die. I wish I would die right now," Carissa sobbed.

"I don't hate you. I just feel a little disappointed. I mean, if you knew your mom might spread the story, then why tell her?" Kevin asked.

"We were talking. I was telling her how wonderful you were, and one thing led to another, and I blurted it all out. I told her how you helped with the food drive and organizing the dance, and how you reached out to Matson. I mean you do so many good things, and then I let it out how much you've overcome," Carissa wailed. "I wouldn't have told her everything, but when I mentioned your dad died in prison, she just wheedled all the rest out of me. . . . I am so ashamed Kevin. You trusted me and I let you down. You're the last person in the world I'd want to hurt . . ."

"Carissa, I know you say your mom is a gossip, but are you *sure* she told anybody about my father?" Kevin asked.

"I'm not one hundred percent sure, but Marko seems to know something and how else could he find out?" Carissa said.

"Did you ask your mom if she told anybody?" Kevin asked. "Because Marko could be just faking it."

"She'd never admit it, Kevin. She'd just lie. She tells her friends all kinds of personal stuff about Dad, and, when he calls her on it, she lies and lies."

"Well, let's hope she didn't tell anybody," Kevin said.

"Kevin, I'm so sorry," Clarissa wept. "I wouldn't blame you if you never spoke to me again."

Kevin briefly hugged Carissa and said, "We'll work it out. It's not the end of the world."

As Kevin was leaving the apartment, he saw Carissa's mother leaning over a porch railing and talking to a woman on the sidewalk. Kevin recognized the woman right away, and she recognized Kevin.

"Hello Kevin," Nattie Harvey greeted him.

"Hi Mrs. Harvey," Kevin answered, a chill going through his body.

"Wasn't that a lovely school dance, Kevin?" Mrs. Harvey asked sweetly.

"Yeah," Kevin said, hurrying on. When

he was out of earshot, Mrs. Harvey began talking in an animated way as both women looked after Kevin.

One time Kevin's grandmother cautioned him about gossip. "Gossip is like you take a pillow full of feathers up atop a windy hill and you let them all fly, and then you want to get them back, but no way can you ever get them back. Those feathers go every which way, and that's like gossip and gossip hurts people and causes pain and you can't take it back," she advised.

Depression swept Kevin. He knew now he should have never opened up to Carissa. He felt so close to her that he wanted her to know everything about him. She should not have told her mother, but Kevin knew his was the first mistake. Now Nattie Harvey was sending her feathers all over, and eventually everybody at Tubman would know. In the meantime, Marko knew and he was trying to take Kevin down, bit by bit. He had already cost Kevin the 100-meter dash.

Kevin turned the problem over and over in his mind. He could always deny everything. Nobody had any solid evidence. Kevin could say Carissa got the story mixed up. By now, the story Carissa told her mother was probably changed anyway. Probably Kevin's father had been turned into Public Enemy Number One who had died in a hail of police bullets.

Kevin could just laugh it off, but he swore to himself a long time ago that he would not lie about his father. He would tell the plain, honest truth that his mother had told him.

At school on Monday, Kevin felt as if everybody was looking at him and snickering behind his back or, even worse, pitying him. He was afraid to look back for fear of seeing shock on somebody's face. After American History I, Jaris Spain called out to him. "Hey Kevin, you got a minute?" Jaris was a nice guy. Kevin liked him.

"Yeah," Kevin said cautiously. Was Jaris going to ask him now? "Is it really true? Surely it can't be true."

"Kevin, you ever hang at Pastor Bromley's church?" Jaris asked.

"My grandparents go there," Kevin answered. What was this leading up to? As the son of a murderer, should Kevin perhaps look for Pastor Bromley's guidance so that he doesn't follow a similar path in life.

"Well, they got a thing going, a bunch of boys from foster homes—ten-, eleven-year-olds. We're giving them sort of a fun day Saturday. Hotcakes and breakfast sausage in the church parking lot, a day at the zoo, burgers in the afternoon. Each kid needs an older guy to kind of be his buddy. You interested?" Jaris asked.

Kevin breathed a sigh of relief. "Yeah sure. You can sign me up," he agreed.

"Matson Malloy came up with the idea. It's no big deal. Just provides some fun and companionship to the little guys," Jaris explained. "Thanks Kevin. I knew we could count on you."

Marko Lane came walking up. "What are you guys up to?" he asked.

156

Jaris gave Kevin a look. Then he told Marko about the program. "These younger kids are like troublemakers already, huh?" Marko mocked. "And Pastor Bromley is trying to get them back on the straight and narrow. Hallelujah!"

"No, the kids are from foster homes," Jaris said.

Marko glanced at Kevin. "You ever been in trouble with the law, Walker? Ever been in juvie? You seem like the kind of guy who'd—"

"We're kinda busy," Jaris said, cutting Marko off.

"Yeah, don't you have anything better to do?" Kevin snapped. "Like sticking your head in a trash bin or something."

"Oooooo, he's touchy. You don't want to get him mad, Jaris. It's in his blood. I'll tell you about that sometime." Marko walked off whistling.

Jaris looked after Marko, a puzzled look on his face. "Well, anyway, see you Saturday about seven. The girls are going to help with the breakfast. It should be fun," he said.

Late in the day, as Kevin went to his locker to put away his English book, he noticed four students already there staring at a note pinned to the locker. One of them was Sami Archer.

The note was written in large, bright red marker letters. It was a crude limerick.

"There once was a killer's son,
Ashamed of the deed Daddy done,
The truth he did hide, he lied and he lied,
But you cannot forever run."

Kevin turned numb. The four students were looking at him, as if waiting for an explanation.

"Twister, what's this?" Sami asked. "Somebody's idea of a joke? It sure ain't funny."

"Marko Lane," Kevin explained. "He's got a sick sense of humor. He wants to shake me up so he can beat me in the meets." Kevin tore the note down and bunched it up. He stuffed it in his pocket. He walked down the hall, his heart pounding.

He had to teach Marko Lane a lesson he would never forget. He had to. There was no more getting around it. Marko usually went across the street for a burger after school. Then he walked home through a field. Sometimes Tyron walked with him, but not on Mondays.

Today was Monday.

Kevin was stronger than Marko. He weighed about ten pounds more, and he was a little taller. Kevin had no doubt he could take Marko down if they went at it hand to hand. He could get Marko down in the dirt and make him understand that he had to stop—or else. It was now the only way Kevin saw to stop the harassment.

Kevin's heart was beating hard as he waited for Marko to emerge from the burger stand and start his walk home. Kevin planned to shake Marko up good. He would not take it as far as he'd gone with Buck

Sanders. Kevin could control his temper better now than he did then.

Kevin waited, growing impatient. He thought about his father. He recalled the photographs of the muscled young man in the boxing ring. Kevin wondered again what had driven his father to that fateful fight. It must have been some terrible provocation. His father must have felt like Kevin did now. There was no way to avoid it. No way.

Kevin thought of all the times since he came to Tubman High when Marko had harassed him. It was as if Marko knew from the beginning that he had the power to harm Kevin. Marko seemed to know there was something vulnerable about the boy from Texas . . . and poor old Mr. Pippin . . . and shy, clumsy Matson . . . and all the overweight, the strange looking, the different ones.

Marko needed a lesson. He needed to go down, with his sneering, brutal face in the dust. He needed to ache in every bone in his body from the beating Kevin would give him. He needed to be afraid.

Kevin had to be the one to do it. And the field was the place. If Kevin did it at school he'd be suspended. Out in the field, he could do what needed to be done, and only Kevin and Marko would know what happened. And Marko would be too ashamed to admit how badly he'd been beaten, how he'd been forced to plead for mercy on his knees.

Kevin was growing excited. When he ran, his hands were open, but now they closed into fists, as if getting ready for the task ahead. He felt the adrenalin rising in his body. He would come up behind Marko and say, "You piece of trash. You have got to be stopped and I'm the one to do it. I'm going to teach you a lesson you'll never forget." Kevin wouldn't jump Marko from behind. No, he would face him and demand that they fight. "You coward, you come on now and show me what you got, and I'll show you what I got," he would dare. If Marko tried to run, Kevin planned to over-take him and force the fight on him.

Marko would not get away this time.

The years seemed to vanish in Kevin's mind, and he was not only Kevin Walker, a sixteen-year-old junior at Tubman High School. He was Charlie Walker, twenty something, big and strong, father of a three-year-old boy, full of anger and righteous rage. He had been wronged and this was the showdown.

He was Charlie Walker, not a brutal man, but a decent man under most circumstances, a gentle man who carried his child on his shoulders and patiently described the names of the colorful flowers they came across. But he was a man who was done with being pushed around. He would be less than a man now if he did not fight, and so he would.

And he took the other man on, and they fought hand to hand until the other man fell into the curb and lay there with his blood spilling into the street. His head was broken open, and he never got up again.

But it wasn't Charlie Walker's fault. The man he killed by accident had driven him too far, and he had no choice but to fight. He just meant to teach the man a little respect. Sometimes a man has to fight. You can't just keep taking it, or you are not a man at all.

Marko Lane finally came out of the burger joint. The sun was going down. It had been a cloudy day, and there would be a red sunset, with streaks of red and gold in the sky.

Kevin watched Marko swagger down the street, heading for his usual trip home through the field. He had hurt and insulted a fair share of his fellow human beings today. He had once again ruined Mr. Pippin's English class. He had pasted that hideous limerick on Kevin's locker. He had laughed at Derrick Shaw for being stupid and at Sami Archer for being overweight.

And now it would end in the field. That's where it would happen. That's where Kevin would put a stop to all the harassment, all the bullying. Kevin remembered the first time Marko Lane had almost tripped him. They didn't even know each other's names. That was the beginning. Today would be the end.

CHAPTER TEN

Kevin followed Marko at a distance.

He hurried his step when Marko got too far ahead. Kevin's heart felt like a large bird in his chest, trying to escape. His eyes narrowed. His mouth was dry. He felt nothing but hatred.

"Twister! No!" came a soft, haunting voice.

Kevin spun around, looking all around him. Had Carissa followed him? How would she know he was following Marko today? How would she know what he had in mind? Kevin saw nothing but the lacy branches of the old pepper trees.

Kevin moved ahead.

"Twister! No!" The voice came again, numbing him. He turned and saw no one. It had to be Carissa. She was the only girl around Tubman who called him Twister.

Then the feeling left Kevin's legs. He dropped to his knees. He felt sick. He was shaking, and the perspiration leaked into his clothing and made a glossy film on his face. He felt as if a great, roaring fever had overtaken him, and suddenly it broke. He knelt there until he had strength enough to get up.

And then, slowly, Kevin recognized the voice. He reached into his wallet with trembling hands. He drew out her picture. Somehow she had managed to reach him. She was always in his heart and on his mind, and somehow, before he made a terrible mistake, she had gotten through to him.

"Mom!" Kevin whispered, tears running down his face.

Kevin scarcely slept that night. Nor did he sleep the nights that followed until it was Friday night, and he dreaded going to Pastor Bromley's church and meeting up with some kid who needed guidance. Kevin didn't feel qualified to guide anybody. But he had promised to go and he would. Some little eleven-year-old boy was hoping for a fun day to interrupt his bleak existence. He depended on Kevin to make it happen, even though he didn't know Kevin at all.

The next Saturday, Kevin arrived early at the church. He saw most of his friends there. He didn't see Carissa and that saddened him. The girls were setting up the tables for the pancake breakfast. The boys were waiting for the bus that would bring the little boys.

Kevin stood there for a moment and watched all his friends, hurrying around, giving up their Saturday for a bunch of strange kids. They were good people. Kevin was glad to have friends like that. But he wondered—would they all still want to be his friend when they found out the truth about him?

Kevin was paired with an eleven-year-old boy named Shawne. He lived at a foster home since his mother, his sole parent, was killed in a car accident. He was a shy boy who reminded Kevin of himself when he was that age.

On their way to the zoo, Kevin asked Shawne if he liked animals.

"Yeah, I like wild animals," Shawne replied.

"When I lived in Texas my mom and I used to camp out, and there were coyotes in the mountains. They'd howl at the moon," Kevin told him.

"Whoa! I'd like that. I never heard no coyote," Shawne exclaimed.

"We got coyotes in the hills around here. About ten miles away," Kevin said.

"I'd like to sleep in a sleeping bag and listen to the coyotes and cook by the fire and stuff. I never done that," Shawne said.

"And maybe somebody would tell ghost stories and that'd be more fun."

Kevin thought that, if today worked out well, maybe they could plan a camping trip for these kids.

At the zoo they saw elephants and tigers and even the pandas, which were the pride of the zoo. "This is a cool zoo," Shawne commented. "I hate where the animals are in little cages and stuff. Here most of them are like in the wild."

"I feel the same way," Kevin agreed. "One time when I was small, somebody gave me a little canary and a cage to keep him in. He looked so sad, I just let him fly away. Maybe he didn't make it out in the wild, but at least he got to be free for a while."

On the way back to the church they stopped at a restaurant, and Shawne ordered the biggest hamburger on the menu. He was a skinny little guy and Kevin figured he could use the calories.

"I had fun today," Shawne said.

"Me too. Do you like the place where you live, Shawne?" Kevin asked.

"It's okay. They don't have no other kids. But I got friends at school. At first I didn't. I felt funny with other kids. I'm kinda scrawny and sometimes I say dumb things. Sometimes my stomach acts up, and I make a bad smell, you know? So you know what I did? I told these guys at school that I'm kinda shy and skinny and I'm not really smart, and sometimes I fart and my sneakers stink, but I'd still like to be their friend," Shawne explained.

"What did your friends say to that?" Kevin asked.

Shawne grinned. "They liked me anyway," he replied.

When the Tubman students said good-bye to the younger boys and put them on the bus, Kevin and the others joined in the cleanup. He told Jaris about planning a camping trip. "Yeah, good idea!" Jaris exclaimed. "My little guy would love that too."

Kevin glanced around at his friends, and the old nervousness came over him. Did they all know? Did some of them know bits and pieces of his secret?

And then Kevin remembered what Shawne had said: "They liked me anyway." Maybe telling everybody the truth was the best way. Maybe the right thing to do was just to be up front and let the chips fall where they may. And your friends might surprise you by liking you anyway.

When the cleanup was finished, Kevin looked at his friends and asked, "Would you guys all sort of gather around? There's something I need to tell you."

They all stood around him, some looking puzzled and others not so much. Alonee smiled as if she knew and wanted to give Kevin encouragement.

"You guys, you're all my friends and I want you to know something. I haven't been up front about everything since I came to Tubman. Well, I didn't know how you'd feel about things. I guess I was scared. And then some of the story leaked out and I want you to know the truth."

"That fool Marko Lane been saying your whole family is bad," Sami said scornfully. "He was talkin' trash—that you're just like your daddy, like those crazy Roman emperors where bad blood ran in the family. I told him to shove it, that's what I told him."

Sami's comment broke the ice, but it still wasn't easy. Kevin looked at the faces of his friends and started to say what he had to say. "When I was three years old, my father killed a man in a fight. My father wasn't a bad man. But he had a bad temper. He went to prison for second-degree murder. I was too young to know him well, but I remember him taking me to the park, carrying me on his shoulders. He never got mad around the house. He was nice to Mom and me. He loved us. But if somebody was treating him unfairly, he exploded like a firecracker. When he was fighting this man, the man hit his head and died. When I was six, there was a riot at the prison and my father was killed. I didn't want to share any of this for fear of how some people would look at me, I guess. I think . . . I was scared and maybe ashamed. So that's it. That's the truth. Marko Lane found out about it, and he's been using it to try to hurt me."

There was a brief silence when Kevin finished talking. Then Sami came up to Kevin and gave him a big hug. Alonee followed.

One by one, they came up to Kevin. Some hugged him. Some shook his hand. Nobody said much. They just hugged him, shook his hand, patted him on the back, or high-fived him. The gestures were so heartfelt that there was no need for words.

Then, slowly, the group broke up and did the final chores to restore the church parking lot to how it was when they arrived in the morning.

Kevin smiled to himself and thought about little Shawne. He had told his would-be friends everything, and, as he said, "They liked me anyway." Shawne was right.

Kevin's only regret was that Carissa had not come. He wished she had been here to see with her own eyes that she had not hurt Kevin by revealing his secret. She wouldn't have had to feel guilty anymore. She would have seen that Kevin's friends did not care about what his father had done many years ago.

Kevin walked over to Carissa's apartment in the early evening. He went up the stairs and rang the bell. This time Carissa's mother was not home, and Carissa was alone because her father was working late.

When Carissa did not open the door immediately, Kevin called out, "Carissa, please open up. I have good news."

Finally, she opened the door.

"Kevin," Carissa said sadly.

"May I come in?" he asked.

Carissa stepped back and let him in. "I didn't even want to go to school," she said. "A couple kids called me and said there was terrible rumors all over the school and it was awful. I felt so bad I wanted to crawl in a hole and never come out."

"Carissa, everything is okay. I told all my friends the whole truth about my father. They were wonderful. They gave me hugs and high fives, and it was beautiful. You don't have to feel bad anymore, Carissa," Kevin consoled her. "You know something? For all these years I've been hiding what happened to my father. My family thought that was a good idea because they were sad and ashamed about his prison record. It was like a big dark secret, a burden on my shoulders. It made me feel like I wasn't quite as good as anybody else. But now everything is okay. I feel free of a big burden."

"Oh Kevin . . . are you sure?" Carissa asked. "You were so popular at Tubman. You were like the biggest thing that ever happened at Tubman. I was so afraid all that would be different if people knew. I mean, I thought things would never be the same and it was my fault."

"Carissa, come back to school. I'm telling you, it's okay. It's better than okay. Everything is cool," Kevin said. He reached out and pulled Carissa against himself, gently stroking her back.

"You're for sure not mad at me, Kevin?" Carissa asked in a wavering voice.

"No. I'm not mad at you. I could never be mad at you," Kevin responded, tilting her head and kissing the tip of her nose. "Marko tried to make a big thing of my secret, but it ended up just proving what a creep he is. For a while there, I was really mad at him. I almost had it out with him, but . . . *something* stopped me. So it's really okay babe. I promise you."

The next day a few students who didn't know Kevin well asked him if it was true that his father had killed someone. Or was that story just a lie that Marko was spreading to undermine Kevin? Kevin patiently explained the truth, and his answers seemed to satisfy everyone. The rumors died out as quickly as they had begun, and in days everybody was talking about the upcoming track meet, which was to be held on the Tubman High campus.

Coach Curry announced the lineup for the meet against Garfield. Given Kevin's bad showing in the last 100-meter dash, Kevin wondered if Curry would ask him to skip the event. But Coach Curry told Kevin he was in the event, as well as in the relay race.

Kevin was determined to make this track meet his best ever. Marko's lame jibes no longer even annoyed him. The air had gone out of Marko's attacks. He was now a clown, dancing around the edges of Kevin's world, powerless to have any effect on Kevin.

Tubman High was wild with excitement as the buses brought the Garfield Giants track team and as cars and vans carrying Garfield fans arrived. It was the biggest meet of the season, and, if Tubman won, it would put them in line for the championship regional games.

CHAPTER TEN

Kevin stood there looking at all his friends in the stands, grinning and waving. They had handmade signs saying, "Go Twister!" Carissa had the biggest, most impressive sign, and she and Alonee were holding it. "We love you, Twister! Go Titans!" it read in gold letters.

As Kevin was scanning the crowd, he caught his breath. Slowly making their way into the stands were his grandparents. They had never seen him run at Tubman or in any of the other schools. Grandma was helping Grandpa to their places in the stadium. Once seated, they got out their binoculars and grinned when they spotted Kevin. Both of them waved, and Kevin waved back wildly.

At the start of the 100-meter dash, Kevin crouched and waited for the signal to go. At the starting gun, he felt strong as he took off, springing from the blocks. He had never started this fast. Usually he lagged at the start and overtook the competition. Today he was flying for the whole

100 meters. He could hear the screams and the chants of the crowd as he broke a record, making the dash in 10.3 seconds.

When the relay team got ready to run, Kevin was again the anchor. Marko Lane started and Trevor was second, with Matson third. Kevin was glad he would not be taking the baton from Marko. Kevin ran the anchor lap the fastest he had ever run, giving the victory to the Tubman Titans in an amazing 55 seconds.

Coach Curry said that the winner of the Arthur Ashe Athletic and Leadership Trophy would be announced at the end of school on Friday. Curry pointed out that the trophy was named for Ashe not only because he was a great athlete but also "because he was a great human being. He helped the less fortunate. When faced with a devastating disease, he continued to reach out to others with courage and compassion."

Marko Lane's father made a substantial donation to the athletic department early in the week. Marko began to smile again with confidence. He thought that the donation would make a difference when the award was made.

Kevin was in his English class when the announcement came across the loud-speaker.

"Silence," Mr. Pippin said. "Here comes the very important announcement." This time the whole class obeyed. Marko reached over and grasped his girlfriend Jasmine's hand. He winked at her. All that new sports equipment in the gym courtesy of the Lane family would surely count for something.

Coach Curry came on the PA system. "I wish to thank all the fine Tubman High School athletes who have contributed to our season. I wish especially to thank the track team, our marvelous Titans, who have given the school our first regional championship. It gives me great joy to single out one special athlete who not only excelled on the playing field, but who has given of himself in many school activities and projects. The Arthur Ashe Athletic and Leadership trophy goes to a young man who, like Ashe, has a heart as great as his talent: Kevin Walker."

As the words sank in, Kevin looked around at the other kids in the class, who were cheering and clapping. Kevin could hear cheers and applause from other class-rooms nearby. He knew his grandparents would jump for joy when he told them the great news. And he knew Mom knew already because she was always with him. And he knew he had a school full of wonderful new friends who accepted and liked him just as he was. Finally, he had nothing to hide. He was just another kid in the class—a boy called Twister.